# An Accidental Adventure

## WE ARE NOT
## EATEN BY YAKS

# AN ACCIDENTAL ADVENTURE

## WE ARE NOT EATEN BY YAKS

**C. ALEXANDER LONDON**

With art by JONNY DUDDLE

SCHOLASTIC INC.
New York  Toronto  London  Auckland
Sydney  Mexico City  New Delhi  Hong Kong

ISBN 978-0-545-39813-8

Copyright © 2011 by C. Alexander London.
All rights reserved. Published by Scholastic Inc.,
557 Broadway, New York, NY 10012, by arrangement with
Philomel Books, a division of Penguin Young Readers Group,
a member of Penguin Group (USA) Inc. SCHOLASTIC and
associated logos are trademarks and/or registered
trademarks of Scholastic Inc.

12 11 10 9 8 7 6 5 4 3 2 1          11 12 13 14 15 16/0

Printed in the U.S.A.                    75

First Scholastic printing, September 2011

Edited by Jill Santopolo
Design by Semadar Megged
Text set in Trump Mediaeval

*To Getting Lost*

"I am averse to writing about adventures, for I dislike them."

—ROY C. ANDREWS,
*Arctic explorer and president of the
Explorers Club from 1931 to 1934*

# CONTENTS

# An Accidental Adventure
## WE ARE NOT EATEN BY YAKS

# 1

# WE MEET THE RELUCTANT RESIDENTS

**IF YOU DID NOT KNOW** what business took place inside Number Seven East Seventy-fourth Street, you might look up from the sidewalk toward the light flickering in an upper window. You might see two eleven-year-olds pass by that window, their faces pale and thin, with dark circles around their eyes, and you might imagine that they are the lonely and neglected children of wealthy socialites, forever trying to escape from their dull and pointless days.

But you'd be wrong.

Number Seven East Seventy-fourth Street is home to the old and exclusive Explorers Club, which is the most important society of adventurers, explorers, daredevils and globe-trekkers in the world. The two children who sometimes pass by the windows are reluctant residents of the 4½th floor of this club, and it is their story which concerns us here.

Now, most children would love to live on the 4½th floor of the Explorers Club. Most children would thrill to learn the mysteries and secrets shared among the explorers, and most children would love spending every evening hearing tales of danger and distant lands from the adventurers, explorers, daredevils and globe-trekkers who passed through those grand halls.

At least, that's what the adventurers, explorers, daredevils and globe-trekkers kept telling the Navel Twins.

Celia and Oliver Navel, it must be said, are *not* most children. They did not like mysteries or secrets, tales of danger and distant lands, nor did they like adventures or exploring, and certainly they *hated* trekking the globe. While other boys might have turned green with envy because Oliver Navel had celebrated his ninth birthday in a cursed graveyard on the edge of the Sahara Desert, Oliver turned green with a stomachache because of the sweet-and-sour caterpillar cake he was served, which tastes even grosser than it sounds.

And while most girls might have screamed with jealousy that Celia had been given a Mongolian pony for her sixth birthday, Celia could not stand the smell of horses. In fairness, I believe that the horse could not stand the smell of her either. Whatever the case, the horse had to be returned to Mongolia with a formal apology from the Explorers Club, and Celia Navel was banned from ever entering the country, which suited her just fine. She did not like wild animals or exotic places. Nor did her brother.

The Navel Twins liked television.

They liked television more than anything else in the world. They would watch for hours and hours without a break, and it didn't even matter what they were watching as long as the comforting glow of the TV flickered across their eyeballs.

That little box contained worlds! Nature shows gave them nature. Dramas gave them drama. And cartoons about talking llamas gave them talking llamas, which one could hardly find in the "real" world anyway. They never wanted to miss a show for anything as boring as school, or dinner parties or going outside to play, and definitely not for trips to places like Mongolia.

Unfortunately for them, Oliver and Celia lived at the Explorers Club with their parents, Dr. and Dr. Navel. Well, they actually only lived with their father, Dr. Navel, as their mother, Dr. Navel, had gone off to find the Lost Library of Alexandria, which she believed had never been lost, and had, herself, unfortunately been lost in the process. Though a search party searched for her, no trace had yet been found. Two of the explorers sent to find her even disappeared themselves.

Sometimes, when there was nothing to do during commercial breaks for one of their shows, the twins would talk about their mother.

"You ever miss her?" Oliver would ask his sister, popping cheese puffs into his mouth like it was no big deal, but really holding his breath for his sister's answer. Looking at Celia was almost like looking at a picture of his mother. Celia had the same little nose and giant eyes. She had the same pale skin and dark hair. Oliver had a face more like his father's, but his hair and eyes were the exact same as his sister's. Both of them had dark circles under their eyes from staring at the screen all the time.

"It's her own fault," said Celia. "If she'd just stayed home with us, she'd never have gotten lost."

"Yeah, but don't you think—"

"Shhh," Celia cut him off, "*Ten Ton Taco Challenge* is back on."

Oliver didn't say anything after that, because he loved *Ten Ton Taco Challenge* and because he could tell his sister didn't like talking about their mother. Oliver secretly missed his mother a lot. Celia's secret was that she hated *Ten Ton Taco Challenge*. She was only watching it now because the sound of frying tortillas kept her from thinking about the Saturday morning their mother left.

"Good-bye, Oliver," she had said. "Good-bye, Celia." She kissed them each on the forehead.

"Uhuh," both kids grunted because cartoons were on and they did not appreciate interruptions. It was hours before they even noticed their mother had gone and taken her big backpack with her. She was always going off somewhere. That was the thing with having explorers for parents.

They were always coming and going, looking for the Ancient City of This or the Lost Library of That. Oliver and Celia could not have known that that kiss on the forehead was the last time they would see her.

Some kids might have taken a lesson from that, and stopped watching so much television, but not Oliver and Celia. After their mother left, they watched even more. A television could do a lot of what a mom did, anyway, like telling stories and keeping them company when they were lonely. And even better, if they got tired of it, they could just turn it off, which you couldn't do with a mom at all. Of course, they never did get tired of TV. It drove their father crazy.

"Too much television rots your brain!" he complained. He was standing in his usual spot behind the couch with his arms crossed in their usual upset way.

"No," Celia answered without looking away from the screen. "Mongolian Horse Fever rots your brain."

Dr. Navel sighed. Celia was right of course. She'd caught Mongolian Horse Fever from that horse he gave her for her sixth birthday. They'd barely gotten her to the hospital in time.

"Well," he said, changing the subject. "We have a dinner to go to. It's in honor of your mother."

The twins stood slowly. They couldn't argue with him about their mother. *Ten Ton Taco Challenge* would have to go on without them.

"Another banquet," Celia groaned.

"There will be a prince, and a hot-air balloonist, and a deep-sea diver," Dr. Navel said excitedly.

"Ugh," Oliver and Celia said together and deflated like two hot-air balloons crashing into the sea.

# 2

# WE HAVE AN
# UNBEARABLE BANQUET

**PLEASE TAKE NOTE** that the activities of the Explorers Club are as secret as they are exciting, and take care not to discuss the affairs we are about to witness too loudly or in the company of those who love to gossip or appear on afternoon talk shows. We who love adventure have a special privilege to witness the calamity, the disasters and the dangers that befall Oliver and Celia Navel, who would have much preferred to be left out of this story altogether. Too bad for them.

Every year for the past three years, the Explorers Club held a grand dinner on the anniversary of their mother's disappearance, and every year for the past three years Oliver and Celia were the only children sitting at the long banquet table under the stuffy portraits of old explorers. In fact, for their entire lives, they were *always* the only children at the Explorers Club.

Their parents held the prestigious title "Explorers-in-Residence," which meant that their whole family lived at the club. They went to all the speeches and lectures and dinners at the club, and Oliver and Celia often had to go with their father to make new discoveries around the world so that they wouldn't lose their prestigious title and get kicked out onto the street. Finding a new apartment that could fit all of their parents' collected artifacts, like cursed arrowheads and medieval torture devices, would be very difficult.

Their mother's disappearance made keeping the job even harder for their father. He and his wife had always been a team, and explorers who disappeared never kept a good reputation for long.

"Perhaps she got lost in a good book," Edmund S. Titheltorpe-Schmidt III joked once the food had been served. He popped a greasy chunk of alligator potpie into his mouth and laughed uproariously at his own joke.

The twins had never liked alligator potpie, nor did they like Edmund S. Titheltorpe-Schmidt III, or Sir Edmund as he (thankfully) insisted on being called. His wealth paid for missions of exploration all over the world, though he usually only used the discoveries to make himself richer. He bragged about having dinner at the White House and Buckingham Palace and the summer residence of King Faisal of Saudi Arabia. Rumors said that he had bought his membership in the Explorers Club, rather than earning it by climbing Mount Everest or discovering ancient ruins.

"I wish we could sell him our membership," Celia grumbled to Oliver. She hated that she was missing the best TV hours of the day for this stupid dinner.

Sir Edmund also claimed to be an expert in cryptozoology, the study of mythical, rare and fantastical animals. He claimed to have a master's degree in cryptozoology from Oxford University, but he had never shown anyone his diploma.

In spite of his wealth, his powerful friends, and his dubious degree, Sir Edmund was a very short man. He was always glaring into the children's faces with his bushy red mustache and his breath that smelled like boiled carrots and stale feet. Or like stale carrots and boiled feet. The twins could not decide.

"I do not know how such a family as the Navels could hold the title Explorers-in-Residence," he complained as they settled in for the main course of the dinner: Nigerian monkey curry, "when one of them has not managed to explore her way home after three years. Perhaps it is time for them to relinquish the title to a more qualified explorer."

"If only," muttered Oliver to his sister.

"Then we could live in a normal house," whispered Celia. "And we wouldn't have to miss the best shows to go to stupid dinners."

They both sighed at the thought. They longed for a life with cable television and without the endless Explorers Banquets. It was the day before summer vacation. They shouldn't have to get dressed up and listen to adults argue.

"My wife," Dr. Navel said to Sir Edmund, "is on the trail of the greatest source of ancient knowledge in the universe. The Library of Alexandria held thousands of documents from all over the world: books of magic and power and priceless objects and treasures. No one knows what became of its wonders when it burned down. Finding out will take some time. And until then"—he smiled at his children next to him—"we will be brave and wait patiently for her return."

The twins' mother had always thought that the Great Library had simply been misplaced, like a pair of glasses or a set of keys, and that it was waiting patiently to be found and put back to use. She had believed this even though everyone else in the world did not.

The twins believed the *Masterpiece Showcase* movie they saw about it that said that the library and its thousands of books, scrolls and artifacts were destroyed in a fire two thousand years ago. The idea that all its mysteries had been hidden someplace else for all those years seemed crazy.

Oliver wondered who would want to find something after all that time. He once found a sandwich he'd left at the bottom of his locker for the whole school year. It smelled terrible and had somehow grown fur. Explorers, though, were obsessed with old lost things, the older and more lost the better. They never seemed to mind the smells.

"I hope you will not go off searching for the Easter bunny, Dr. Navel," Sir Edmund sneered at the twins' father. "What would become of your poor children?"

His sudden explosion of laughter made the Navel Twins wince and shift nervously in their seats.

"I'm reminded of Colonel Percy Fawcett." He chewed loudly while he talked. "Colonel Fawcett disappeared into the Amazon in nineteen twenty-five looking for the Lost City of Z. Did you know that he took his oldest child, Jack, with him? I imagine they fell victim to cannibals or venomous snakes. At least your mother had the good sense to *abandon*—excuse me, I mean *leave* you safely at home." He took a big gulp of his sickly sweet Ethiopian honey wine. "Don't worry, children," he said, and smiled. "If your father misplaces himself like your mother did, I would take responsibility for your upbringing *personally*." He laughed again and stuffed another stringy piece of monkey meat into his mouth. Oliver had never thought of the word *personally* as a curse word before, but the way Sir Edmund said it made his skin crawl.

"I wonder if he has cable," Celia whispered to her brother.

"He's not even an explorer," their father said to himself while Sir Edmund banged on his glass to get the waiter to bring him more honey wine. "He's a businessman and a . . . a . . . a *charlatan*!"

The children had to assume from their father's tone that it was a terrible thing to be a businessman or a charlatan, let alone both at the same time. Even if they didn't know what a charlatan was (and who does?), for their part, being an explorer wasn't so grand either. It had cost them their mother and no end of headaches.

"What's a charlatan?" Oliver asked his sister.

She didn't answer him. She didn't want their father to think she cared about any of this explorer nonsense. She also didn't know and didn't like to admit when she didn't know something. She was three minutes and forty-two seconds older and that meant her brother had to respect her the way a younger brother should.

"It means a faker, a liar and a fraud," Sir Edmund said. "And though there may be a charlatan at this table, I promise that it is not me."

Oliver couldn't believe that Sir Edmund had heard him. Though he was tiny and looked ridiculous with his big red mustache, he was dangerously clever and had really good hearing.

The twins ate the rest of their dinner in silence. Their last day of fifth grade was tomorrow and once that was over, summer vacation would finally start. They looked forward to three months of doing nothing but watching television and learning as little as they could. Starting middle school in the fall would be enough of an adventure for them.

During the school year they had to do homework and go to classes, and take "educational field trips" with their father, which usually ended up with them getting lost in ancient mazes of doom or in Oliver getting bitten by a newly discovered lizard.

It had happened.

Twice.

The first time, the bite made his skin turn purple and everything smell like old bananas for a week. The second time, his skin turned green and his whole body ached, even his hair. Again, everything smelled like bananas. And Oliver hated bananas.

Their teachers often objected to the classes

they missed, but their father ignored the objections.

"Adventure is the greatest source of education," he always said.

Their classmates objected, wishing they could go off with a famous explorer instead of sitting through vocabulary lessons and filling in bubbles on multiple-choice tests.

"Wish you could go in our place," the twins always said. Adventure, in their opinion, was more fun to watch from the sofa than to experience.

During the school year, aside from being forced to take dangerous trips to exotic lands, they only got to watch two or three hours of TV every day, which they thought was far too little.

Every winter they dreamed of entire summer days spent in front of their programs, and every summer their father interfered with their plans.

They hoped this summer would be different. They were eleven now, going into the sixth grade, and wanted to take control of their destiny and their television. The dinner party was already messing up their plans.

The conversation had finally moved on from

talking about their mom. Their father was talking to an African prince about ancient pygmy myths, and Sir Edmund was lecturing everyone on his side of the table about the difficulties of hunting mythical creatures. He claimed to have captured bigfoot and sold him to the president of a Canadian mining company. All the explorers, adventurers, daredevils, globe-trekkers and businessmen at the table were fascinated.

Oliver and Celia, as usual, were not.

"The key with mythic creatures," Sir Edmund explained, "is to find their weaknesses. For some it's food. Others, like the yeti—or abominable snowman, as you might call it—love musical theater and have an almost fanatic devotion to their children." He winked at the twins. "Still others only want to taste human flesh. Keeping such creatures in a zoo is, I must say, an expensive challenge, but one I very much enjoy. Bigfoot, the abominable snowman, the basilisk . . . my zoo-keepers are never bored."

"Zoos," Celia sighed. She could imagine nothing more boring than watching a bunch of caged animals—mythical or not—sleeping and eating and sniffing each other. Oliver secretly wondered what you fed an abominable snowman, but he was afraid that if he asked, the answer would take hours and hours. Explorers love to talk. Celia would kill him if Oliver made the dinner take any longer than it already was. They both wanted to get the night over with and get through the last day of school.

After another hour of chatter about venomous *this* and ancient *that*, they were finally excused from the dinner table. They rushed out of the room to get back to their apartment on the 4½th floor.

Their father hardly noticed that the twins were leaving. He was too engrossed in a story the African prince was telling him about poisonous plants of the Ituri Forest, but Sir Edmund watched them go.

If they had been paying any attention to him at all, they would have seen him smiling at them with cruelty in his eyes, as if he knew something terrible about their future and was enjoying the thought immensely. And truth be told, he did and he was.

# 3

# WE GET NO LOVE
# AND NO BEARS

**"WHY DON'T YOU GO** downstairs to meet Choden Thordup, the Tibetan mountain climber?" their father asked, standing behind the sofa where his children lounged in front of the TV.

It was the day after the banquet. They had made it through the last day of school . . . somehow. Kids were bouncing off the walls, excited about summer baseball leagues and summer camps and summer vacations. They peppered Oliver and Celia with questions:

"Where are you going this time?"

"Will you go skydiving?"

"Will you fight a monster?"

"Will you meet a king?"

All the other kids imagined that life must be

so wonderfully exciting for the children of world-famous explorers.

"We're going to watch *reality shows*!" Oliver answered excitedly.

"And *soap operas*!" Celia practically squealed. The other kids fell into disappointed silence.

"Weirdos," they muttered as they walked away.

"If I had parents like theirs, I'd never want to watch TV!"

Oliver and Celia just shrugged. They didn't have a lot of friends. It didn't bother them, especially not now that they'd made it home and summer had finally begun.

But here was their father, already trying to interrupt their plans.

"She can tell you about the top of the world!" Their father's excitement caused his little round glasses to fall off his face, but his excitement was not catching. "She's spoken to the Great Oracle of Tibet! She survived the Poison Witches of the Tsangpo Gorge with nothing but her wits . . . and a recipe for spicy mashed potatoes!"

"*The World's Greatest Animal Chases Three* is coming on," Oliver answered flatly.

"Why watch reality TV when *reality* itself is so

much more exciting?" Dr. Navel threw his hands up in the air. He sounded just like the kids at school. He sounded like the teachers too.

"*Love at 30,000 Feet* is not reality television," Celia corrected her father. "It's about an airline crew."

"We're watching *Animal Chases Three*!" Oliver argued.

"Are not," Celia answered. "*Love at 30,000 Feet*. Captain Sinclair is going to confess his love for the Duchess in Business Class."

"A bear is going to race a hippo!"

"Love!"

"Bears!"

"Love!"

"Bears!"

"Enough!" their father bellowed. "There are more important things in life than love and bears— I mean, than television." He flipped a switch and the screen went dark with a disappointed hum.

"Hey!" both children shouted in harmony. "We were watching that."

"Nope. Now you're going downstairs to hear her tales of the Tsangpo Gorge, the Roof of the World and the Great Oracle of Tibet."

"We don't want to hear about some fortune-teller," Celia complained.

"The Great Oracle of Tibet is much more than a fortune-teller, Celia. This is a once-in-a-lifetime opportunity."

"But you say that every night!" objected Oliver.

"And it's true every night. Now, Oliver, put on your jacket and tie."

"But—"

"Celia, your dress."

"But—"

"No more *buts* or the TV goes away for the rest of your summer vacation." The children made their best sad puppy faces at their father.

"Choden Thordup is one of only a handful of explorers to have ever seen the Hidden Falls and survived," he said, smiling and trying to get his kids excited again. It didn't work and his smile vanished. They were not interested in waterfalls. "I swear, when I was your age, if I had had half the opportunities for excitement you two have, well . . ." He shook his head sadly. "I'll see you downstairs in ten minutes. Tonight, you will attend the Ceremony of Discovery."

"*Dad!*" both children shouted, but it was too

late. Their father was out the door and heading down the stairs to the Great Hall.

The children groaned and made their way to their rooms so they could get dressed. Their hopes for a carefree summer in front of the TV were falling apart. They would once again be subjected to tales of adventure and intrigue in distant lands.

When they emerged from their rooms, uncomfortable in their fancy clothes, they stood frozen in the hallway, neither one wanting to be the first to move for the door. Oliver tugged at the tie around his neck. Celia yanked on the pleats of her dress.

"I hate the Ceremony of Discovery," Oliver lamented.

"It's like public television only you can't change the channel," Celia said.

"Dad never lets us do what we want," Oliver complained.

"It's *our* summer vacation. We should be able to watch whatever we want."

"I bet he wishes he had different kids."

"Kids who like adventures."

"Kids who want to climb mountains and get bitten by lizards."

"Kids who aren't us."

They both stood in silence for a moment, staring at the dark TV screen, imagining what they were missing.

"That settles it," said Celia.

"It does?" asked Oliver.

"Yes, it does," she said. "We are going to run away, so that Dad can get new kids and so we won't have to go on any more adventures."

"But isn't running away an adventure?"

"Not if we go somewhere dull, like an orphanage or a children's prison. Any giant, boring place that has cable."

"Oh," Oliver said, because he never could win an argument with his sister and he did want cable television. "What about Dad? He'll be all alone."

"*The Daytime Doctor* said that people need to move through the stages of grief so they can have full lives," Celia explained.

"I don't want to move anywhere," said Oliver.

"Me neither. That's the point."

"All these scientists," complained Oliver. "They always want you to deal with your baggage too. I don't want to pack baggage ever again."

"So we agree then?"

"What? About *The Daytime Doctor*? I don't really like talk shows."

"No! About running away so that Dad can move through the stages of grief and find children who want to handle baggage and stuff."

"Oh," Oliver said again. His sister always got him to agree with her on things. She had a way of talking that was like a trap. You listened and didn't know where it was going. It sounded normal, but then suddenly, before you knew it, you'd agreed to watch *Love at 30,000 Feet* or *Amores Enchiladas* on the Spanish Channel way up in the high numbers. Even if you ended up learning Spanish, it wasn't worth it. *Amores Enchiladas* was a boring show where the women were crying all the time, if they weren't kissing some tan sword fighter guy.

But as usual, he agreed. Celia was three minutes and forty-two seconds older and one and five-eighths inches taller, which gave her a kind of authority.

It was decided: They would run away somewhere dull and watch their shows and everyone would be happier. Children's prison couldn't be worse than the Explorers Club, could it?

# 4

# WE DEBATE DEATH AND CABLE

**THE EXPLORERS CLUB** is an old building filled with many mysteries, as old buildings tend to be. This old building contained countless secret doors and tunnels and places to explore, as befitted its name.

Celia and Oliver had discovered the network of secret tunnels by accident. They had once lost the fancy universal remote control that worked on any device made in the last ten years, if you could just figure out which button to press. They looked for it under cushions and on top of cabinets and eventually behind a small bookcase. They did not find the remote control. They found a tunnel, and that tunnel led someplace else. They weren't sure where because neither of them wanted to explore it. They kept looking for the remote, which Oliver had left in his sock drawer for reasons he could not remember.

So there the tunnel sat, unexplored by the incurious children until the moment they decided to run away. As much as they hated the idea of using the tunnel, they couldn't exactly stroll out through the front door of the club with all the explorers around. They had to be sneaky.

Celia grabbed the small canvas backpack that her mother had given her a few years ago.

"We'll need supplies," she explained as she tossed a bag of cheese puffs into it. Oliver grabbed the remote control. He never could figure out what all the buttons did, but he would have plenty of time in prison or the orphanage to try to figure it out. It might even make him popular with the other inmates. He'd be the guy who could control the TV from anywhere. He liked the idea. If he were a superhero, he'd be the Channel Changer. Celia threw in a *TV Guide*, because she liked to know what was on all the time. She also made them each throw in their pajamas.

"Ready?" she asked.

"Ready," said Oliver.

"Okay, then. Here we go."

They sighed with longing for the episodes of *Love at 30,000 Feet* and *The World's Greatest Animal Chases Three* they were missing, and took one more look around the apartment.

They saw the Cabinet of Count Vladomir, a medieval torture box that their parents discovered in the ruins of a French castle on their first date. They used it for hanging coats. It was next to the refrigerator. Count Vladomir would not have been pleased.

They saw their father's collection of antique pipes from around the world and their mother's drawings of exotic birds. Oliver hesitated when he saw the storyboard from the movie *Escape from the Mummy King*, hanging behind the couch. It was a set of illustrations that movie directors use to tell their story before they start filming it. The storyboard looked like a page from a comic book. *Escape from the Mummy King* was based on a story their mother had written in *National Geographic* magazine. She got the director to give the drawing to Oliver and Celia after the movie finished filming. It was one of their most prized possessions. Oliver thought about bringing it.

"Come on," Celia said, and shoved her brother

into the tunnel ahead of her, leaving the story-board and their miserably exciting lives behind. She insisted on carrying the backpack. Oliver had a way of losing whatever was handed to him. She shut the entrance behind them.

The tunnel was dark and the direction unknown. There was a weird symbol carved on the wall every few feet. It was like an old key and it had odd letters below it in some strange language. Explorers loved weird symbols and strange languages, the weirder and stranger the better. This one looked familiar to Celia for some reason, but she couldn't figure out why. Not that it mattered. Soon they wouldn't have to think about explorers ever again.

They crawled for what seemed like hours, each one of them silently imagining the television shows they were missing at that exact moment and wondering if they had made the right decision. Their father would be down at the ceremony won-dering where they were. They hadn't even left a note. Somewhere in the distance, a rat scurried. Oliver nearly screamed. He hated rats. Every time his sister's hand brushed his ankle, he thought it was a rat.

"Watch it!"

"Move faster! Don't be such a sissy."

"Don't be such a jerk." He stopped and she slammed into him.

"Ouch!" they both said.

They continued on in silence, angry already, and regretting their decision to run away. But neither of them wanted to back down first. And they certainly couldn't just go back. That would mean sitting through the Ceremony of Discovery, and maybe losing their television privileges because they were late, and even worse, probably getting dragged on some exotic trip that their father thought would inspire them. Fiji, or maybe Antarctica.

"Do you know where we're going?"

"Just trust me," said Celia. "And keep crawling."

Oliver had his doubts, but his sister was confident and her confidence made him feel better. She had that female intuition their father talked about. "Women just know things, son," he would say. "Trust them and you will go far in life."

Oliver thought about his mother. How good could her intuition be if she was still lost looking for the Lost Library of Alexandria? But what if she wasn't lost at all? What if she had left because she didn't like her boring children and wanted to go on her own adventures without them? Did she regret leaving them? Would she come back now that the twins were gone? Maybe running away really was for the best.

His thoughts were interrupted by a thud on his head.

"Ouch," he said, and stopped. His sister smacked into him again.

"Ouch," she said too. "Why'd you stop?"

"Wall."

"Is it a dead end?"

"I can't see. It's too dark."

"Can you push on it?"

"I didn't try."

"Well, try!"

Oliver tried and the wall moved. It swung open into a dim room. They crawled out of the opening and closed it behind them as they brushed layers and layers of dust off themselves. They were so dusty, they looked like ghosts.

They were in the club's library. The library was a big room with high ceilings and stained glass windows. Bookshelves went up as high as they could see and wooden ladders with brass fittings crisscrossed the shelves so that people could reach all the books. Their mother had always told them that it was nothing compared to the Lost Library of Alexandria.

"There were grand halls that could hold thousands of volumes, lecture halls and quiet nooks to study in. The greatest thinkers in the world discussed philosophy and science at every turn. They measured the world with their minds, decoded the stars. They discovered unknown species and they recorded great and terrible prophecies. They collected everything, from treasure and magic to unusual hats. The catalog alone filled a thousand tablets in a room the size of a circus tent!"

Their mother had a way of making libraries sound important and exciting. She even made library *catalogs* sound important and exciting. A giant room filled with thousands of tablets sounded a lot more interesting than a list of books.

There was nothing exciting about the Explorers Club library. There were old leather chairs where the explorers liked to smoke cigars, and crusty old books with names like *Endurance!* and *A Gift to Those Who Contemplate the Wonders of Cities and the Marvels of Traveling.* There was an old card catalog that listed all the books, which no one but the librarian knew how to use. A fire burned in the fireplace. The librarian often threw sage into the fire to fill the room with a more pleasing smell, and to chase away bad spirits. There wasn't any sage in the fireplace now, though. The librarian had gone off to the ceremony downstairs.

But if the librarian had gone, why was the fireplace still lit?

Both children turned to each other, wondering the same thing at the same time, when the doors burst open. They ducked quickly behind a large marble statue that stood by the wall. It was tall and thin and made out of a bright green jade. It looked like a giant toothpick.

Celia pressed Oliver against the statue with her whole body, trying to get as flat as possible. His face was smushed against a large brass plaque that read IN MEMORY OF FRANK PFEFFER & JANICE MCDERMOTT, THE GREAT DISCOVERERS OF THE JADE TOOTHPICKS. YOU STILL OWE US MONEY. COME BACK SOON.

The statue was built in honor of the final tragic Pfeffer/McDermott expedition. Frank Pfeffer and

Janice McDermott, discoverers of the Jade Toothpicks, went to China to look for Oliver and Celia's mother a year ago and never returned. No one ever heard from them again. Explorers had a way of disappearing.

"Ouch," Oliver whispered. "You're crushing the word *toothpicks* into my face."

"Shhhhh . . ."

"Who gets famous for discovering toothpicks?"

"*Explorers*," Celia snapped, with a roll of her eyes. "Now, hush or they'll hear us." Ducked behind the monument, the twins couldn't see who had come into the library, but they could hear.

"Everything is ready," a woman said. "They will never expect us."

"They better not."

The children recognized the second voice. They would know it anywhere. It was Sir Edmund. Celia peeked out, but all she could see was the back of a chair and Sir Edmund's feet dangling down. They didn't even reach the floor. She couldn't see the woman.

"If you do not live up to your end of the bargain, the Council will be most upset," Sir Edmund said.

"The Council should have more faith. This time, we cannot fail."

"I have heard that from you before."

"Will Navel uncover the truth?" she asked.

"Only as much as we wish him to uncover," sneered Sir Edmund.

"He is clever."

"And for now, that is useful. No one could lead us to the discovery better."

"Except his wife," the woman said, and it was clear from her tone she did not like their mother.

"Mom?" Oliver whispered. Celia pressed her finger to her lips telling Oliver to be quiet.

"Yes," growled Sir Edmund. "Except his wife."

"What if Dr. Navel suspects something before we . . ."

"He will *not*!" Sir Edmund shouted, then regained control of himself. "Don't worry. You do your part and we cannot fail. When he is no longer useful to us, he will be destroyed."

"And the children?"

"Those brats will come to me," said Sir Edmund. "You may not harm them permanently."

"Whatever you say," the woman responded. "We won't harm them . . . permanently. I can't imagine why you would want to look after them. Children are such a bother."

"If I give them cable, they'll not cause any trouble," Sir Edmund said. "I hate the television, but it does keep their mouths shut. And I believe they will one day be useful to me."

"Fine," the woman said. "As long as Navel can be controlled. The letter makes it seem that he might be the one who—"

"The Navel family will be taken care of. I want to hear no more about it. Now we must be going before anyone notices our absence. And remember to do your part."

"Of course I will. And you, Edmund, mind your tone. I don't work for the Council."

"My tone? Ha!" Sir Edmund really seemed to enjoy being a jerk.

Oliver and Celia heard footsteps across the floor and then heard the giant library door slam shut again. They were finally alone.

"Who was that woman?"

"What did she mean that she won't harm us *permanently*?!" Oliver asked.

"I don't know. Sir Edmund shouldn't have called us brats."

"He wants to destroy Dad!"

"And give us *cable*," Celia added. "Cable!"

"Hmmmm." They both considered the situation. On the one hand, there was a plot afoot against their father. On the other hand—cable! But their father would be "destroyed." The twins both knew what that meant. Out of the picture. Toast. Dead.

"We have to warn Dad," Oliver said at last.

"Yeah," Celia agreed. "We'll run away another time, once Dad is safe."

"Maybe if we save Dad's life, *he'll* get us cable," Oliver suggested as they made their way, still covered in dust, to the Great Hall, where the Ceremony of Discovery was in full swing.

# 5

# WE DECLARE A DISCOVERY

**THE CEREMONY OF DISCOVERY** is a time-honored tradition of the Explorers Club. Every month, explorers, celebrities, professors and businessmen of enough importance to receive an invitation gather at the club to hear speeches about the newest and most exciting discoveries. There were always a few charlatans in the crowd too, trying to act like they belonged there.

It was at this ceremony in 1909 that Dr. Frederick A. Cook declared that he was the first explorer to set foot at the North Pole, and it was also that same night that Robert Peary declared that *he* was the first explorer to set foot at the North Pole.

A great feud broke out over who had indeed arrived at the North Pole first. They accused each other of faking their journals, of making up data and telling tall tales. They challenged each other to duels, and sent their supporters to pick fights with the opposition outside the National Geographic Society. A small group of Inuit hunters, the original Arctic citizens, meanwhile, had been visiting the North Pole for over a thousand years, but none of the explorers asked their opinion on the Peary-Cook feud.

"The Inuit tend not to keep journals," Dr. Navel explained when he told the twins about the feud as a bedtime story. "Their legends and their memories are the maps that guide them. They leave the bragging and the journals to explorers."

"I think I prefer the Inuit way of doing things," Celia said. Their father laughed and kissed her on the forehead.

"Just like your mother," he said sadly.

Oliver and Celia crept along the hall, nervous that they might run into Sir Edmund or his mysterious companion. As they got closer, they could hear the clinking of glasses and the loud chatter of the explorers at the Ceremony of Discovery. They eased themselves along the walls slowly. How would they explain being so dirty? They hoped they could just warn their father about the plot on his life, get him to give them cable, and get back out again before anyone made them listen to some tale about mountain climbing.

"Ready?" asked Celia when they reached the door to the Great Hall. "Remember, move quickly and try not to look suspicious."

"How do I do that?"

"Act confident!"

"But I'm not confident!"

"That's why it's called acting, dummy." And with that, she grabbed her brother by the ear and shoved him into the room first.

As they stood, frozen side by side in the doorway of the Great Hall, no one so much as looked at them. Though they were covered in dust and grime, and carrying a backpack, the children were hardly the most bizarre-looking people in the room.

Professor Eckhart of the Department of Obscure Spiritualities at the University of Norôurárdalur in Iceland wore his gray hair in a mohawk. He also had a monkey on his shoulder. Madame Xpertina, a famous trans-Siberian motocross rider, wore her hair in a purple buzz cut and had on an outfit made of shining black leather. She appeared to be chatting with a naval officer who had a kangaroo on a leash. There were soldiers in uniform and businessmen in tuxedos and scientists and athletes and at least two astronauts in the room, all dressed up and chattering away, clutching glasses of sherry. The very smell of sherry made Oliver's stomach turn. Celia had never bothered so much as to smell it.

A remarkable trait of Celia's, it should be noted, is that she lacked all curiosity. She did not like to know how things worked, how they smelled, what they tasted like, why they were made, who made them, or where or when. She wanted only to be left alone to watch her programs. Oliver felt the same way, but for a different reason. Curiosity always ended with him covered in lizard bites.

The walls of the Great Hall were hung with the heads and pelts of animals. A full-size cheetah, frozen mid-leap, was mounted on a platform in the center of the room. A collection of birds perched eternally on the rafters. Elk, deer and buffalo heads watched over the gala with lifelike glass eyes. Near the door stood a polar bear on its hind legs, its mouth open in a growl and its paws raised to attack.

Sometimes Oliver and Celia felt like they, too, were part of the club's collection of treasures, and that they would end up mounted on the wall of the Great Hall one day, with ghastly expressions on their faces and marbles instead of eyes.

More disturbing for Oliver and Celia, though, was the stage at the opposite end of the room that was used for the endless slide shows and speeches that the explorers liked to give. The idea made them shiver, but they harnessed their courage for their father's sake and for the hope of getting cable.

Dr. Navel, dressed sharply in a tuxedo, saw his children standing in the entrance to the Great Hall. He wrinkled his forehead a moment at their dusty clothes and their small backpack, but then just shrugged and motioned for them to come over to where he stood with three other men, listening to a woman dressed in colorful, flowing robes tell a tale. The children, scowling, approached.

". . . and there was the Great Oracle, the ferocious spirit of Dorjee Drakden, eternal protector of the Tibetan people, waving his sword over his head like an ancient Tibetan warrior," she said. This was the mountain climber their father had been so excited to meet.

"Dad," Celia whispered, tugging at her father's tuxedo jacket.

"Shhh." He swatted her hand away. She tugged again. He swatted her again and gave her one of those looks that parents must learn from some book. She let go of his tuxedo.

"What do we do?" mouthed Oliver to his sister, trying not to attract too much attention. Celia scratched her head while she thought and raised a small cloud of dust.

"The oracle growled and hissed." The mountain climber was still telling her story. "His spirit was wearing the body of a little monk like a costume, making him do things that would have been impossible for a person to do if he weren't possessed by the Oracle. His robes twirled, and his sword whistled through the air and stopped a hair's width from my throat!"

She spun and slashed her hands through the air like a sword as she spoke. She winked at Celia, who stared back at her with an expression on her face like she'd just seen an infomercial for hedge clippers. Choden Thordup continued.

"The oracle demanded I prove my courage. He demanded that I jump out the window. We were in a monastery high on the edge of the Tsangpo Gorge, which fell ten thousand feet below us." She paused and let the terror of her situation sink in.

Celia crossed her arms, waiting for the explorer to keep talking. Oliver rolled his eyes. There was nothing dramatic about pauses, he thought. They were like commercial breaks and he wondered why storytellers always insisted on using them. Why didn't she just get to the point? They had to warn their father already.

Oliver decided to interrupt: "Dad, we have to tell you something."

"Not now, Oliver," Dr. Navel said. "What's gotten in to you both? Ms. Thordup is telling a story."

"But it's important!"

"It will have to wait a moment. It is rude to interrupt. I don't interrupt you when you are watching your stories on television."

"Yes you do!" Oliver objected. "All the time!"

"Well, I'm your father and I'm allowed. Now, let Ms. Thordup finish her tale." He turned to the mountain climber. "Apologies. Please, continue."

Oliver shifted from foot to foot while Choden continued.

"The fall would certainly kill me," she said. "Then again, the sword at my throat would certainly kill me too. We needed the oracle's blessing to continue our journey, so I did what any reasonable explorer would have done. I smiled and then flung myself out the window."

Dr. Navel looked at his son and raised his eyebrows, trying to show how impressive it all was, but Oliver just stared back with the same expression a cow might have, had it been invited to a Ceremony of Discovery at the Explorers Club.

He was wondering if it was worth enduring the rest of this story to warn their father. Maybe they should have run away, if this was how they were to be treated when they had important news. Celia crossed her arms and tapped her foot impatiently. Sir Edmund was probably somewhere in the crowd putting his plans into motion and their father cared more about some mountain climber falling out a window. Celia felt that this was a deep injustice. Missing TV, finding out devious plots, and now, listening to long stories about Tibet! On TV, warnings were given much faster. No one ever had to listen to speeches on *Love at 30,000 Feet* unless they were really important.

"Dad, there's a plot to destroy—" Celia tried to say, but the mountain climber just kept talking over her.

"I landed on a wild yak, sixty feet below," Choden continued, ignoring the twins. Their father's face was growing red with anger while he tried to act like he also hadn't noticed his children's outbursts. "Yaks are amazingly strong creatures and their thick fur makes for a soft landing. I rode the yak back up to the monastery, where the oracle was laughing hysterically. He told me that the yak was his gift to me. He then left the body of the monk he had possessed, who collapsed, rigid, to the floor. We named the yak Stephen, and I later donated him to the Denver Zoo."

The men laughed. The children did not, even though it is hard to keep a straight face when someone says the word *yak* over and over again.

"I don't believe I've had the pleasure of meeting you yet," the climber said, finally turning to Oliver and Celia. "What are your names?"

"Celia," said Celia.

"And Oliver," said Oliver.

"My name is Choden Thordup," said Choden Thordup, pointing to her name tag. "As you probably guessed, I'm a mountain climber. Are you interested in mountains?"

"No," Celia answered for both of them.

"We're not," Oliver added for both of them too. He didn't like that his sister always tried to get in the last word. And the first word, for that matter.

"You must be undersea explorers then." Choden smiled.

"Nope."

"Astronauts?" she tried, still smiling.

"No."

"Jungle trekkers?"

"No."

"Egyptologists? Botanists? Geographers?"

"We don't like to go anywhere," Celia said.

"Or do anything," Oliver added.

Choden Thordup's smile vanished, as did Dr. Navel's.

"Well, I see, umm . . . ," Choden said after a long and uncomfortable pause. The children just stared at her. Her face turned red.

"Can we talk to our father now?" Celia snapped. "It's a little more important than yaks."

"Well," Choden said, and smiled too nicely. "I have to tell your father something too, so why don't you just wait a pretty little minute? Young people in my country are *never* allowed to interrupt adults. They must learn patience."

Explorers are a special kind of adult, like magicians and clowns, who hate it when children don't find them fascinating. This one, it appeared, got very mean.

Celia did not like Choden Thordup, and neither did Oliver. Their father was shooting daggers at them with his eyes. Oliver and Celia couldn't believe it. They were trying to save his life and he thought they were being rude!

"Dr. Navel." Choden turned to him. "After leaving the monastery, I descended to the rapid river in the gorge below. The gorge is one of the last unexplored regions on earth. No one knows who or *what* lives down there. I hoped I might find Shangri-La in its depths."

"Shangri-La!" exclaimed Professor Eckhart. "Such a place is only a legend."

"Perhaps," said the mountain climber. "But in my travels, I stumbled upon the remains of a temple behind a giant waterfall. The building, built inside a cave, had been burned, but in the ruins, I found this."

She pulled a clear plastic folder from under her dress. In it was a piece of parchment that looked very old. It was covered with symbols and strange writing. The writing looked a lot like the weird writing from the walls of the tunnel behind the bookcase in Oliver and Celia's apartment. The edges of the parchment were black where the fire had touched them.

"I believe this is a piece of—"

"The Lost Tablets of Alexandria!" Dr. Navel interrupted, gasping, and no longer looking at his children. Suddenly, the room went silent and all heads turned toward him. "From the Lost Library itself."

"And there's another thing," said Choden Thordup, turning the document over to reveal the back. It was covered in small, neat letters, written in light blue ink.

When he saw it, Dr. Navel gasped and dropped his sherry glass to the floor, where it shattered.

# 6

# WE WITNESS A WAGER

DR. NAVEL TOOK the plastic folder from the mountain climber and studied it carefully, as the whole room got quiet.

"This is my *wife's* handwriting," he said. Oliver and Celia looked at each other, stunned. For a second, they forgot all about the plot to destroy their father.

"I do not know the language on the paper," explained Choden Thordup. "But the image at the top of the page is clearly the seal of Alexander the Great. Your wife, thankfully, wrote in English on the back."

"Mom?" Oliver mouthed at Celia, who just shook her head with confusion. They had both seen their father get excited about clues before. He'd dragged them all over the world looking for their mother, and it never led to anything but long flights, animal attacks, missed television, lizard bites and disappointment. Celia just couldn't get too excited about some old piece of paper. And Oliver got his hopes up way too easily. Sometimes Celia felt like she was three years older than her brother, rather than three minutes and forty-two seconds.

"The language is ancient Greek," Dr. Navel pointed out, and Celia managed to see strange letters and weird symbols curling around each other.

For years, she'd heard her father say the phrase "it's all Greek to me" when he didn't understand something, and now she knew what he meant. The symbols didn't look like any letters Celia knew. She couldn't understand them at all.

"*Mega biblion, mega kakon*,'" Dr. Navel read out loud.

Ancient Greek, we should note, wasn't "all Greek" to Dr. Navel. He understood it perfectly, as any decent explorer would.

"Big books, big evil!" said Dr. Navel. "A statement by the famous Callimachus."

"Who is Callimachus?" Oliver asked, and his sister glared at him. Her brother was already distracted from the point of coming to the ceremony—to warn their father and to get cable.

"He was a scholar at the Library of Alexandria," Dr. Navel said. "He invented the first classification system in the world. He organized all the knowledge in the library—which was written on these tablets. The Lost Tablets are the catalog of the Great Library—a complete account of all its wonders. They were created back before the library was lost."

"That doesn't look like a tablet," Oliver said.

"Well, they called them tablets," Dr. Navel answered, "but they really used parchment to write them. It wouldn't have been practical to carve new tablets for every book and scroll. The library was far too big. It held all the knowledge in the world."

"Ugh," Celia groaned. "We have to hear about librarians now? This is worse than school! Worse than afternoon public television! Dad, we have to warn you about—"

"Callimachus had a feud with the other scholars in Alexandria," Dr. Navel continued, thinking out loud and not hearing a word his daughter was trying to say. "Some said he was part of a secret society that was trying to take over the library and seal it off from the world, but no proof has ever been found."

"Why was he a librarian if he thought big books were evil? Why would he want to seal it off?" Oliver wondered, and then saw his sister glaring at him again. "You know, as if I cared," he added.

"That is an excellent question," Dr. Navel said, thrilled his son was taking an interest. Their mother always said that their father had "selective hearing." Celia never knew what that meant until now. "Callimachus was from the noble class, and he hated the idea of common people having access to all that knowledge. Knowledge is power, after all, and all the knowledge in the world would mean all the power in the world. Callimachus thought that that power should be kept for only a few—"

"Dad," Celia interrupted, because she just didn't care about ancient librarians. "We have to warn you about—"

"Look at what your wife says," Choden Thordup interrupted Celia, who was getting really sick of being ignored.

Dr. Navel ignored Celia too. He also forgot what

he was talking about, and immediately flipped the page over to look at his wife's handwriting. He read aloud what she had written:

" 'November fourth'—She wrote the date! We know when she was there!" he said, as if it were the most exciting news in the world. " 'November fourth, little time left; they are close behind me, letting me search for the missing pages until they strike'—She was being chased!" Dr. Navel looked around the room to see if anyone else shared his concern, but all the explorers wanted to hear was what she said about that parchment. " 'I'm closer now than I've imagined. No one thought the Great Library might be in Shangri-La. Only the shamans' eyes can tell the way from here.' " Dr. Navel fell silent for a moment. "That's all she wrote," he sighed. "She did some strange sketches of skeletons and demons and things. . . . I've never seen anything like them before."

"What's going on?" Oliver whispered to his sister.

"Don't ask me," she whispered back. "I'm supposed to be watching the Duchess in Business Class tango with Captain Sinclair."

"I hate dancing," Oliver said. "And I'm hungry."

*Celebrity Whisk Warriors* would just be coming on after *The World's Greatest Animal Chases Three*. It was one of Oliver's favorites. Celebrities had to make exotic meals for famous chefs in dangerous situations. The best meal cooked with the fewest injuries won money for charity.

*Celebrity Whisk Warriors* reminded him of his mother, who loved to cook, though she always made weird things like roasted caterpillar pie or scorpion soufflé. Oliver was getting really hungry just thinking about food, and all this was taking too long. He craved fried chicken and strawberry shortcake, or an ice cream sundae and cheese puffs. His mouth watered, but he didn't dare eat any of the food the waiters were carrying on trays. It was all weird things his mother would have liked.

"All right, Dad!" Celia finally said, fed up with how long it was taking to tell their father that someone wanted him dead. These things should really be easier to do. "We *have* to tell you something!"

"Not now, Celia!" Dr. Navel snapped. "Can't

you see that your mother might have made the greatest discovery of the past two thousand years? She might have found Shangri-La and the Lost Library at the same time!"

*"But Sir Edmund is trying to kill you!"* Celia shouted.

The room went silent for what felt like forever.

"Can we get cable now?" Oliver muttered, staring down at his feet.

"What?" said Dr. Navel.

"Can we get cable?" Oliver repeated quietly.

"We heard Sir Edmund plotting to kill you," said Celia. "And we thought if we warned you, we could get cable installed in the apartment."

*"Nonsense!"* a voice from the crowd shouted.

No one could see where the voice came from.

*"Lies!"* the voice called again, and everyone looked down to see Sir Edmund as he stepped into the conversation, wagging his finger into the air.

He wore a black tuxedo with a frilly ruffled shirt. His jacket had decorative bands on the shoulders, like a military officer's, and he wore a gold medal on his chest emblazoned with an emblem of a scroll locked in chains. The chains were encrusted with jewels and they sparkled right into the children's eyes.

"Your children have seen too many movies."

"I agree with you," said Dr. Navel, "but I do wonder why they would make this up. I have never known them to imagine anything at all before."

"Because they are brats," Sir Edmund said. "And they believe too much in fiction. It must run in the family," he sneered. "This document could not possibly be from the Lost Library of Alexandria. The tablets are as lost as the library itself. And there is no such place as Shangri-La. If you believe in this foolishness, you are as foolish as your foolish children."

"I do wonder," said Dr. Navel, turning back to the mountain climber. "If this is indeed a Lost Tablet from the Great Library of Alexandria, how did it get into Tibet? Who are these *shamans* my wife mentions? And who was chasing her? And, of course, where are the rest of the Lost Tablets? What do her drawings mean? Where is Shangri-La? So many questions . . ."

"Excuse me!" Sir Edmund called up at Dr. Navel. "I said you are a fool!"

"Yes," Dr. Navel replied, "I heard you. I have more important things to do right now than worry about your opinion of me."

"He also threatened to kill you!" Oliver called out, but none of the adults reacted. Threats were nothing new at the Ceremony of Discovery.

"Do you really think Shangri-La could be real?" Professor Eckhart asked.

"Why not?" said Dr. Navel, thinking out loud. "The legend says that there is a secret place somewhere in Tibet called Shangri-La. It is an earthly paradise, hidden and protected from the evils of the world. The monks of Shangri-La safeguard all the wisdom of the universe so that, if humanity ever falls into ruin, all will not be lost. It is possible, I suppose, that when the Great Library was destroyed, some wise scholar could have secreted the tablets away to Tibet. A secret city would be the perfect place to hide a Lost Library."

"This is what I believe," added Choden Thordup excitedly.

"This is ridiculous," Celia said to her brother. "There's a *real* plot to kill Dad and all these explorers can think about is a stupid library catalog and a made-up place hiding a stupid library. I'm missing *Love at 30,000 Feet* for this?"

"No," Oliver said. "You're missing *The World's Greatest Animal Chases Three*. And what if this helps Dad find Mom?"

"What if the Codex of Zanzibar last year helped Dad find Mom?" Celia answered tartly. "Or the trip to the Golden Sarcophagus of Peru or the trek through New Zealand or the deep-sea exploration over winter vacation? There are always clues and they never lead anywhere except to missing our shows and you getting bitten by lizards."

Celia's eyes had welled with tears. Oliver's too. He didn't like it when his twin sister scolded him. But he couldn't help thinking she was right. Except this time, the page had their mother's handwriting on it, didn't it? That clue had to mean something more than any of the others had. But something felt wrong about it. He couldn't figure out what it was, but *something* just didn't feel right.

"Something just doesn't feel right," Celia said. As annoying as it could be to have a twin sister, sometimes it was helpful. Oliver didn't have to say anything. They were thinking the same thing.

There was something not right about Choden Thordup either, for that matter.

Celia thought the Tibetan mountain climber looked the way a person looks when she's just handed in a paper about a book she didn't read. The teacher always says that seeing a movie isn't the same thing, but it's so much more fun to watch the movie, so you do and then you write the paper and you hope that the book and the movie are the same and that the teacher won't notice. Choden Thordup had *that* look on her face. Celia knew *that* look. She was an expert in it.

"Shangri-La is a fantasy," Sir Edmund scoffed. "Only fools believe in it." He looked menacingly at Dr. Navel. Oliver and Celia tried to glare menacingly back at him, but he didn't even seem to notice.

"My wife was no fool," Celia and Oliver's father answered. "She believed in it. I wasn't certain until now, but I believe she found it, which means she was right about the Great Library too. The Lost Tablets are the closest thing we have to finding the library itself."

He held the paper up above Sir Edmund, who did not even bother to look up at it.

"Don't be an idiot, Navel." Sir Edmund rolled his eyes. "You'll get the children's hopes up."

Oliver and Celia looked to their father, who gazed back at them with his gentle blue eyes that held so much sadness. His glasses had slipped down his nose again. He missed their mother, very dearly.

"The scientific value of such a discovery would be unimaginable," he finally answered. "Shangri-La *and* the Lost Tablets of Alexandria!"

"Poppycock!" Sir Edmund shouted.

"I am no liar, sir," Choden Thordup added. "This place is real."

"Rubbish!" said Sir Edmund. "No such thing."

"But the doctor's wife's writing suggests that—"

"Balderdash!" Sir Edmund cut her off.

"You do wrong to insult our guest," Dr. Navel said.

"You do wrong to believe in such a fairy tale. I think this discovery is just a cry for attention from an unknown mountain climber trying to make a name for herself. Who ever heard of Choden Thordup before today?"

The explorers' murmurs got louder, but no one spoke up.

"I've discovered more in my sock drawer than you will ever see in your entire life," Choden Thordup finally answered.

"Name one thing!"

"If we were in my country, Sir Edmund," she snapped, "I would feed you to a yak."

"Yaks don't even eat meat," said Sir Edmund.

"For you, they would make an exception," Choden replied.

Oliver and Celia smirked at each other. This was *almost* as good as a soap opera. Sure, their father's life was in danger—even though he didn't seem to care—and their mother might be found, and threats were flying back and forth across the room like paper airplanes during study hall, but this sort of thing happened every day on television, and you could eat microwave popcorn while you watched it. All the snacks at the Ceremony of Discovery were slimy. Some were still moving.

*"Enough!"* shouted Professor Kamil Rasmali-Greenberg, the president of the Explorers Club and the most legendary adventurer in the world. He had been made a king in several countries, was

called a god in others and had the world's largest collection of ties with ducks on them. He was wearing a thick purple and green one at the moment, and, because he was a very big man, the tie was almost as wide as Celia's head.

"I will not have more arguing than usual at this meeting," the professor announced. "We have now reached eight minutes of shouting and death threats for every one minute of meaningful discussion and that ratio cannot stand. There are two children standing here who are anxious for this gathering to be finished." He winked at Oliver and Celia.

"True explorers do not behave like this," the professor continued. "Unless their reputations are at stake. Therefore . . ." He paused and let his gaze sweep across the room. "I propose we settle this like proper members of this fine institution: *with a wager.*"

Another murmur spread through the room, along with some excited applause. Explorers love a bet, especially one with a risk of death or dismemberment.

"If Dr. Navel can follow his wife's path to Shangri-La and discover the remainder of the Lost

Tablets, he will gain fame and glory for all time," said the professor.

"And if he cannot?" Sir Edmund asked, his voice dripping with contempt.

"If he cannot . . ." Professor Rasmali-Greenberg sighed, uncertain.

"I have a suggestion." Sir Edmund smirked. "If he cannot find the Lost Tablets, he will be banished from the Explorers Club in disgrace . . . forever."

A flurry of whispers and speculation passed through the Great Hall, and all eyes, including those of Celia and Oliver, went to Dr. Navel, who remained calm and cool. A grin crept across his face.

"I'll accept this wager, on one condition," he said. "If I win, Sir Edmund will also pay for the installation of cable television into our apartment."

Oliver and Celia almost cheered.

"I have another condition too, then," Sir Edmund snapped. "If you lose the wager, your children will become my servants."

"Only during vacations," Dr. Navel said. "They have school."

"Every vacation until they are eighteen," Sir Edmund responded. "Even the short ones."

The twins' smiles vanished. Their eyes went wide.

"Daaaaad . . . ," they both said warily, shaking their heads. "Daaaaad?"

"Agreed," said Dr. Navel, and he extended his hand down to Sir Edmund, while Oliver and Celia stood with their mouths hanging open. "A wager is made."

"It is made," Sir Edmund said, reaching up to shake Dr. Navel's hand with a curt snap of his wrist. He leaned in close to Oliver and Celia and sighed. His breath wrinkled their noses. "Your foolish father has doomed you, I'm afraid. This journey will lead you only to despair. A pity."

He turned and left the room abruptly. Other explorers cleared a path for him as he went. The top of his head brushed the bottoms of everyone's sherry glasses, but he held it high and knocked more than one to the floor.

"Dad," Oliver tried again, once Sir Edmund was gone. "We heard him say he wanted to destroy you! What if you've fallen into his trap? And stuck us in it too!"

"Don't be so suspicious, son," Dr. Navel said. "You've seen too many spy movies. Sir Edmund is not nearly clever enough to trick me like that. I've been everywhere from Machu Picchu to Dayton, Ohio. I think I can handle him."

"But Dad," Oliver objected once more. Celia elbowed him in the ribs.

"Shhhhhhh," she whispered. "If Dad wins this bet, we get cable."

"But what if he *loses*?"

"Ms. Thordup," Dr. Navel said to the mountain climber. "I would like very much to question you further about how you came to find this document and what you know of this hidden temple behind the waterfall. Perhaps you can even help us find a guide for the journey." He turned back to Oliver and Celia. "Children, I'm glad to see you are already packed. We will leave for Tibet right away."

"Be careful," Choden said. "The monastery where I found this page was guarded by more than just men. This is the realm of the *Dugmas*—the Poison Witches—and countless unknown terrors. I barely escaped them myself."

"So we will first have to see the Oracle of Dorjee Drakden," Dr. Navel said casually. "For his blessing."

"Wait," Celia gulped. "He's the one with the sword?"

"And the yak?" Oliver spluttered.

"That's the one." Dr. Navel smiled. "How exciting!"

And with that Dr. Navel and the Tibetan mountain climber disappeared toward the map room with the ancient piece of paper. The children stood alone among the explorers in the Great Hall, thinking about cable television and Lost Tablets, and wondering whether or not yaks ate people.

But most of all, they were thinking about their mother.

## 7

# WE HEAR FROM A YAK

**TIBET IS LOCATED** in Central Asia, in the highest region on earth, and getting there isn't easy. On the first part of the flight, Oliver watched three movies and a twenty-minute show about exercises you could do in your seat to keep from getting something called "deep vein thrombosis," which sounded like a kind of musical instrument, but was really a dangerous medical condition. Then they had to change planes in Germany and fly for another eleven hours to get to an airport in China, where they would then fly another two hours to get to the capital city of Tibet, called Lhasa.

Oliver found himself happy to be going on such a long trip. He was happy because the airline had installed personal television screens on the back of every seat, so he could watch whatever he wanted and he had hours and hours to do it. His father didn't complain or suggest Oliver read a book. He didn't even notice that Oliver had been watching movies and television for almost twenty hours straight. Celia had drifted off to sleep after watching some romantic comedies with titles like *Summer's Storm* and *Kissing Cousins*.

Dr. Navel was two rows ahead, madly flipping pages in the books and charts and maps Choden had given him. Occasionally, he would shout "Aha!" and the people around him would shift uncomfortably in their seats.

"Couldn't he just snore or something?" a man behind Dr. Navel said loudly.

Across the aisle from Oliver, Celia muttered in her sleep: "He'syourcousin, don'tmarryhim . . ." She sighed and shifted without waking up.

On his little screen, Oliver was suddenly watching a nature show about mountain wildlife. He liked nature shows, though he thought he'd been watching a movie. These airplane systems were weird, he guessed, changing channels on their own. He didn't mind, though. On nature shows, you could see the entire world without getting bitten by any lizards. And you got to drink the endless supply of soda the airline gave out.

But when a wild yak stared out of the tiny screen at Oliver and said, in an ancient language unheard for over two thousand years, *You will have to remember enduring Love if you want to escape a terrible fate,* Oliver realized, much to his surprise, that he was asleep and dreaming a most unusual dream.

The yak had bright green eyes that looked cold and hard, like the jade statue that Oliver and Celia had hidden behind in the Explorers Club library.

"Why am I dreaming about a yak?" Oliver wondered to himself. "I don't think I was even watching a nature show when I fell asleep."

*Yes you were,* the wild yak with the jade eyes told him.

"No I wasn't," he thought.

*Yes, you were. I'm reading your mind. I know everything. Stop arguing with me or I'll climb out of this screen and eat you.*

"Yaks don't eat meat," Oliver replied.

*Well, then I'll climb out of the screen and skewer you with my horns,* the yak answered.

"Okay," Oliver thought, because it's never a good idea to argue with mind-reading yaks. "How do I understand you? I don't speak any ancient languages."

*How do you know I'm speaking an ancient language?*

"It's my dream. I just know."

*All right. I guess I am speaking an ancient language, but that's not really the point. I'm a yak. I shouldn't be speaking at all.*

"I agree."

*Good. Now that we understand each other, I have a cryptic message for you.*

"What does that mean?"

*Cryptic? It means "serving to camouflage an animal in its natural environment."*

"That doesn't make any sense."

*It also means "having a meaning that is mysterious or obscure."*

"That makes more sense."

*Thank you.*

"You're welcome. So what's the cryptic message?"

*I said it already: You will have to remember*

*enduring Love if you want to escape a terrible fate.*

"What is that supposed to mean?"

*I don't know. It's a cryptic message. I'm just the messenger.*

"Well, who are you carrying the message for?"

*It will be clear in time.*

And with that, Oliver found himself awake, staring at his screen. A movie about a lonely superhero was on. He hadn't been watching a nature show at all. It *was* just a dream.

"Aha! I knew it! The yak was wrong!" he shouted. The people around him looked over nervously. The man in the seat next to Oliver grunted and pushed earplugs into his ears, shaking his head. Across the aisle, Oliver's sister jolted out of her own nap.

"Why are you yelling?" she snapped at him.

"I . . . ummm . . . there was a . . . nothing. Just a dream."

"Well, you didn't have to shout."

Oliver turned the volume up on his headset and acted like he was watching the movie, but he was really thinking about his dream. What could the green-eyed yak have meant? How would remembering enduring love help him? What terrible fate did he need to escape? It really was a cryptic message.

Meanwhile, Celia, now awake from her nap, was feeling sore. She was tired of sitting in the uncomfortable airline seats and tired of traveling and tired of worrying what awaited them high in the mountains of Tibet. The man at the window seat next to her kept shoving her arm off the armrest with his elbow. He was reading a newspaper and wore too much cologne. His nose was red and short and he was wearing a shiny black suit that hadn't wrinkled at all during the long flight. He breathed too loudly through his nose and wouldn't give back the armrest. She shoved at his arm, reclaiming it by force. Without a word he jabbed right back with his elbow and pushed her off again.

"*Ow!*" she shouted. "Stop being a jerk!" The man glared at her and reached up to press the button that summoned the stewardess.

"May I help you?" the stewardess asked, appearing almost instantly. She had the whitest teeth Celia had ever seen, but her skin was caked with makeup, like she'd painted her face with the kind of paint they use for road signs.

"This young lady is being very rude. She has attacked my arm on more than one occasion," he said, smiling at the stewardess and adjusting the lapels on his shiny suit. "Normally, I wouldn't complain, but I worry that this family is troubled. They have all shouted at some point during this otherwise pleasant flight. Her latest outburst was simply the last straw."

"Young lady?" the stewardess asked, raising her eyebrows at Celia, who really didn't know what the question was.

"He pushed me first," she said.

"Where is your father?"

Celia's heart sank as she pointed to her father, who had now asked a small Chinese lady next to him to hold her finger on a point on a big paper map while he measured some distance with a string.

"Hold still, ma'am! Please try to hold very still, otherwise I'm sure we'll find ourselves lost in the Gobi Desert."

"Sir," the stewardess interrupted. "Could I speak to you, please?"

Dr. Navel looked at the Chinese lady, who smiled at him, but used her eyes to plead with the stewardess for help.

"Perhaps we could talk at the back of the plane?" the stewardess suggested. Dr. Navel reluctantly put his maps and strings down on his seat and followed her to the back. Celia watched while the stewardess lectured her father. He had that pose that boys get when they're in trouble. He slumped and shrugged and acted like he wasn't listening. Then the stewardess pointed at Oliver and then at Celia, and Dr. Navel got angry and started lecturing her. And then she got angry and pointed at him. Then she poked him in the chest and out of fairness, he poked her back, which was not a good decision.

"Do not dare touch me, sir!" the stewardess shouted, and everyone turned to look.

"You touched me first," Dr. Navel said sheepishly, realizing he had gone too far.

The stewardess picked up the little phone next to her and spoke into it very quickly. A man stood up from a seat near the front of the plane and walked back toward them. When he passed Celia's seat, she saw him wink at the man in the shiny suit, who gave a quick nod of his head, like they were old friends.

When the man reached Dr. Navel and the stewardess, he pulled out a badge.

"Air marshal," he said. "Is there a problem here?"

"No problem, sir," Dr. Navel said, trying to undo the damage that had already been done.

"He has been a disturbance this entire flight," the stewardess said. "We have reason to believe his children are . . . unbalanced, as he is himself, and now he has assaulted me."

"I did not assault you," Dr. Navel tried to say, and Celia looked at Oliver with worry in her eyes. Oliver's eyes showed worry too.

"We're not *unbalanced*," Oliver whispered, and then thought about the talking yak in his dream.

"Sir," the air marshal said. "Please do not interrupt. Unfortunately, I have been noting your unusual behavior since leaving New York, and I cannot allow you and your family to continue to put this aircraft and its staff in danger."

"I promise we will sit quietly until we land."

"Unfortunately, sir, you cannot be permitted to remain on board."

"What?!"

"You and your family will have to leave the plane."

"But we're forty thousand feet in the air somewhere over Central Asia!"

"Sir, please don't cause a scene," the air marshal said. "We are only at thirty-eight thousand feet, and we are just passing over Mount Everest. It'll be a lovely piece of sightseeing for you." He glanced back at the man next to Celia and smirked. Then he winked at Celia and gave her a thumbs-up, like the whole thing was one big joke. If getting thrown out of an airplane was a joke, she didn't get it.

# 8

# WE FEEL THE GRAVITY OF THE SITUATION

**EXITING AN AIRPLANE IN MIDAIR** is not an easy thing to do, even if you wanted to do it. And the Navel family certainly did not want to do it.

In fact, Celia tried to bite the air marshal's finger when he came to grab her, but the shiny-suited man in the seat next to her grabbed her and held her still while the air marshal tied her hands in front of her. Celia noticed that each man wore a gold ring with a tiny key inscribed on it and the key had tiny shining stones embedded in it.

"If you can't behave, I'll have to leave you restrained," the air marshal said cruelly. "I don't want to do that."

Two of the stewardesses tied Oliver's hands in front of him and moved him to the back of the plane. One of them looked at him and mouthed the words "I'm sorry," but it did little to comfort him. He didn't like heights. He could already taste the dry chicken and soggy strawberry shortcake he'd eaten an hour earlier. It was far less pleasant-tasting going in reverse. He wanted to look brave for his father, so he took deep breaths and kept himself from throwing up. His father, meanwhile, had already been handcuffed to the duty-free shopping cart. He looked pale and his eyes darted frantically, trying to think of a way to save his family from a thirty-eight-thousand-foot fall. His glasses slid down on his nose and he could not get them up again.

This was not the first disaster Oliver and Celia had faced with their father, but it was perhaps the worst. River rapids could be navigated. Wild horses could be calmed. Angry cannibals could be persuaded to go vegetarian for health reasons. There was no arguing with a thirty-eight-thousand-foot fall.

"You're really going to kill us for causing a disturbance?" Dr. Navel asked the air marshal. Some of the other passengers on the plane looked concerned, but no one seemed to want to interfere.

Many people didn't seem concerned at all. They kept staring at their glossy magazines, paperback novels or miniature television screens. Oh, how the twins longed to be back in front of the television at home!

"I'm not going to kill you," the air marshal said. "I am just going to remove you from the plane. What happens after that is up to you . . . and gravity."

"This is crazy," Dr. Navel said to the stewardess.

"You should *not* have poked me," she replied coldly, and dragged the duty-free shopping cart— and Dr. Navel with it—through the door to the tail of the plane. The air marshal shoved the twins after them.

"You can't do this!" Dr. Navel shouted.

"Oh, yes, I can," said the air marshal, and he knocked Dr. Navel on the head. Dr. Navel crumpled to the floor, unconscious. The marshal took off Dr. Navel's handcuffs, untied the children's hands, and, without a word, he and the stewardess left, locking the door that led back to the airplane cabin.

"What happens now?" Celia asked.

"They are going to open the tail and the pressure will suck us out and we'll fall," Oliver said. "I saw this in a movie."

Suddenly, the door opened again, and the stewardess was back.

"Excuse me," she said, smiling like she was interrupting their nap. "Don't forget your carry-on bag." She set Celia and Oliver's small backpack on the floor and left the tail again, locking the door behind her. Celia and Oliver just stared at the door. Oliver ran over and pounded on it a few times, but nothing happened.

"We're in trouble." He leaned against the door and sighed.

"We need parachutes," Celia said, tugging her brother out of his slouch. "Fast."

They scurried around the back of the plane and found a big square of yellow plastic with a string on it.

"What's this?" Oliver pulled at the string. Suddenly, there was a whoosh of sound, and the square unfolded and started to fill with air. It knocked Oliver over as it took its shape: a life raft.

"That's great," Celia said. "If only we were on a boat."

Oliver ran over to the duty-free cart that the stewardess had left behind and pulled out a heavy canvas poncho with the airline's logo on it.

"They're selling these for twenty-three ninety-five," he said. "That's a good deal."

"What are you doing? This isn't the Home Shopping Channel, Oliver! We're about to die!"

"I have an idea," Oliver told his sister excitedly. He pulled out three more of the canvas ponchos and started tying them together by their hoods. Celia saw what he was up to and started to help him. When they ran out of ponchos, they started tying plastic garbage bags to the ponchos. Within a minute, they had a giant canvas and plastic quilt that sort of looked like a parachute.

"I know the movie this idea is from," Celia said anxiously. "Things don't go well, remember?"

"The heroes survive the fall, don't they?"

"Yeah, but they end up eating bugs. I hate eating bugs."

"Don't think about that now. We just need to tie this to the raft somehow," he said. "And get in it quickly."

They found bungee cords and started attaching the patchwork parachute to the raft as fast as they could. Their parents had made them take a survival class every Saturday during kindergarten and they still knew their knots pretty well. Dr. Rasmali-Greenberg had been their teacher. For every knot they learned, he let them watch a half hour of cartoons. Much to his surprise, they learned over a hundred knots and reclaimed their Saturday mornings for *Ducks Incorporated* and *Flappy the Parrot Prince*. They were excellent students when they had the right motivation.

As they tied, they heard a loud clank and the floor started to shift.

"Uh-oh," Oliver said.

"They're opening the hatch," Celia shouted. Daylight began to slice into the dim space and their ears popped. The air roared around them.

"Ouch!" they both shouted. Oliver grabbed his father's feet and Celia grabbed his arms and they tossed him into the raft. He hit his head on the floor when they did it.

"Sorry, Dad," Oliver said, but his father didn't react at all. Celia put on their backpack and then they jumped into the raft themselves and kept working at the knots on their parachute.

"I hope this holds together," Celia said. The raft

started to slide toward the opening at the back of the plane. They saw the clouds far below them.

"Hang on to Dad!" Celia yelled. Oliver grabbed his father by the foot with one hand and held on to the handles of the raft with the other. He sat down on the parachute they'd made so that it wouldn't open up right away. At the speed they were going, the wind would tear it to shreds. He would let it out once they'd fallen a bit. He knew that much from action movies. If he'd had the Discovery Channel, he probably could have made something better, he thought, but it was too late to worry about that now. If they survived, they'd get cable.

Well, if they survived and avoided the Poison Witches and found the Lost Tablets of Alexandria in the land of Shangri-La and won the bet with Sir Edmund. Put like that, it seemed impossible.

Oliver closed his eyes to quiet his thoughts, and felt a rush as the raft with three-fourths of the Navel family slid through the opening and fell out of the airplane.

He heard his sister's high-pitched scream, which was strange, because he opened his eyes and saw that her mouth wasn't open. Then he realized it was his scream and they were falling through the sky.

# 9

# WE SEE A SHUSHING

**ON AN ICY PEAK** high in the mountains of Tibet, a group of men sat in a circle of thrones beneath a giant statue of a ferocious creature with a dozen arms and a dozen snarling heads. Some of the men wore the yellow and maroon robes of Buddhist monks, others were in the black robes of priests and some wore business suits. There was even a man in blue jeans and a T-shirt, with a baseball cap pulled low over his face. Candles flickered in front of the giant statue, casting strange shadows on the walls.

The men watched the floor in the center of their circle, where a man stood in a trance. He wore the sparkling robes and giant banners of the protector-spirit, the warrior-god, Dorjee Drakden. When the spirit entered the man's body, he rose taller in his shoes, his chest puffed and his voice grew loud and deep.

"Who calls me?" he bellowed. Bells at the top of his helmet jingled. He held a shining sword, and his eyes, wide and full of fury, darted around the circle of men. He saw the powerful monks of the Yellow Hat sect sitting on the floor behind him, each frozen in meditation, yet alert to his every move. He saw the priests and the men in suits and the shadows dancing on the walls. The spirit searched for the only being to whom he would bow, the highest lama in Tibetan religion, His Holiness the Dalai Lama.

Dorjee Drakden swung his arms and swept around the circle. He did not see the Dalai Lama; he did not see anyone he considered worthy of his friendship. He arrived at the center of the circle, face to face with a little man on the largest throne, a little man whose feet did not even touch the floor.

"Greetings," Sir Edmund said as the god hissed and snarled in his face. Dorjee Drakden's helmet rose several feet above Sir Edmund and his sword could have easily sliced the little man in two, but Sir Edmund was not alarmed. He snapped his fingers, and immediately, two young monks appeared at his side and gave him a long white scarf, which

he presented to the spirit. "I bring the respect of the Council, and gratitude for your service to us."

"I serve the ancient ways, beyond time and form, beyond good and evil." As the warrior-god spoke, a secretary scribbled every word he said onto a scroll. "I obey no master, but see and hear the crumbling of the universe. I protect the dharma and guide those who stray beyond the hope of kindness. I am fire, light and air. I bow to none but the—"

"Yes, thank you," Sir Edmund interrupted. "That's lovely and we are very glad for you. We've called you here to tell us what we need to know."

"Insolent little man! You dare to speak to me in this way! I spin the Wheel of Protection and bring demons to despair!"

Sir Edmund stood on his throne so that his face was a little above the protector-spirit's.

"In the name of the Council, I demand you answer me, Drakden. You may be immortal, but that little monk who you're living in isn't. He's our prisoner. So tell me: Where is the Navel family? Where have they gone? They were supposed to land in Beijing. Why aren't they on the plane anymore?"

Dorjee Drakden drew back from Sir Edmund and swayed and swooped around the room, hissing and growling, nearly falling under the weight of armor and robes, before stopping in the middle of the circle of men.

"They are out of your control. They fall toward the gorge and the Hidden Falls. Great power is with them, though they know it not. Great evil too!"

"They should have landed in Beijing," Sir Edmund muttered to himself. "This was not the plan. How will our agents intercept them?"

"If someone else finds them," said the man in the baseball cap, while texting on a tiny cell phone, "then your whole plot is in danger of falling apart, Ed."

"My plot is perfect!" Sir Edmund objected. "This is just a wrinkle. My people will come through."

"But if the Navels should find—"

"Relax," said Sir Edmund. "I always have a backup plan. They are headed into the realm of the Poison Witches."

"*Heresy! Damnation!*" shouted Dorjee Drakden as he rushed at Sir Edmund, waving his sword and shouting. "These witches do not respect my authority. They are unholy creatures, whose souls are black and screeching owls. Murderers! They will not bow to me!"

"Oh, hush," Sir Edmund snapped. "Get over yourself. Do you want Shangri-La to be found? Turned into a tourist attraction? An amusement park?"

"I do not," said Dorjee Drakden with a swipe of his sword through the air, trying to regain his impressive composure. "I have protected it since before it existed."

"That doesn't make any sense," Sir Edmund said. "Now stop being cryptic. I need to make sure they find their way to this place."

Sir Edmund pointed to a map on the wall that was unlike any other map in the world. It was old and faded, and would not have been so useful for getting from place to place. It showed the deep valleys and high mountains of Tibet, but it also showed other dimensions, realms of gods and devils, ghosts and saints. There was no north or south or east or west. It was a map of the unseen and the unseeable.

Sir Edmund was pointing to an area that showed a hill with a collection of small round huts. In the center of the huts burned a fire. Wide-eyed ghosts with many heads and many clawing arms scrambled from the flames, tiny versions of the giant statue behind the monks.

Dorjee Drakden looked at the strange map, then yelled and hissed, and with a roar, he tossed his sword at Sir Edmund. The blade spun through the air end over end. Sir Edmund did not move. The blade missed him by centimeters and slammed into the map.

"Their path will lead them to this place, but I will do no more!" he declared.

"Good," Sir Edmund said.

"Except for this," the spirit continued. Sir Edmund rolled his eyes. "I am the Great Oracle and this I prophesy: *The greatest explorers shall be the least. The old ways shall come to nothing, while new visions reveal everything. All that is known will be unknown and what was lost will be found.*"

He finished with a long hiss into Sir Edmund's face, and, with the sound of a gong, the spirit left the monk's body, and he collapsed to the floor. Young monks rushed to him, untying the armor and the helmet, which weighed enough to crush the little monk now that the god no longer filled his body. The monk would be exhausted for days and sleep the soundest sleep of his life, with no memory of the things he said or the dark predictions he made. He would wake up in a prison cell.

The scrolls on which the spirit's words had been written were quickly tied closed and rushed from the room to be copied and hidden in the depths of the monastery, where thousands of years of prophecies were stored.

"We will deal with the Navels first," Sir Edmund said. "This oracle has given me great cause for hope. 'What was lost will be found.' Most excellent for us. The foolish explorer and his dull children have no idea what they're in for. I knew they would do exactly what we wanted. We just have to find them again." He smiled and hopped down from the throne. The other monks looked at each other with worry in their eyes.

"Stop being such cowards," said Sir Edmund. "Dorjee Drakden will do as we ask. What choice does the old god have? He's our prisoner, after all. The Poison Witches will take care of the rest. Trust me. The Lost Library is as good as mine."

"You mean ours, don't you?" an old monk asked.

"Yes, ours. Whatever," sneered Sir Edmund.

# 10

# WE AREN'T EVEN
# AT THE WORST PART

**THERE WAS A ROAR,** a sickening spinning feeling, and a blinding light. For a moment, it felt as if all the air had been sucked out of the children's lungs by a cruel vacuum cleaner. The air was thin that high up, but luckily, they were falling fast toward better air. Unluckily, they were falling fast toward the ground too. From thirty-eight thousand feet even falling into water was like landing on cement. And they were falling toward an icy mountain.

Oliver prayed their do-it-yourself parachute would work. If he and his sister died, he would never get to see what happened in the final season of *Agent Zero*, which was about a teenage super-spy living a complicated double life. Who would turn out to be Agent Zero's real father? Who had planted the bomb in his algebra textbook? Why was Principal Drake talking to the president?

"I need to know the answers if I'm going to have any peace in the afterlife," he thought.

After a moment of screaming and spinning and thinking about missing *Agent Zero*, it didn't feel like they were falling at all. It felt more like they were being pushed up from below, though they were still spinning. They had to hold on tightly to the raft and to their father, and their arms were tiring. Oliver couldn't handle it anymore. He lifted himself off the parachute, letting it fly out from under him. It snapped and twisted in the air. Two or three of the plastic bags broke away and twirled off into the sky. Oliver feared the whole chute would tear to pieces. The knots connecting it to the raft strained, but held. The canvas ponchos stayed tied and the chute filled with air.

"Well, those were worth more than twenty-three ninety-five," Oliver said.

Celia's stomach churned as their fall slowed. They felt themselves jerked upward and then, suddenly, they were drifting. The parachute was working. They weren't falling anymore, at least

not deathly fast. They were floating slowly toward the clouds below them.

"I can't believe that worked!" Celia shouted.

"Me neither," yelled Oliver. They both still held tightly to the raft, though they could now let go of their father, who was still out cold.

As they drifted through the sky, the view was amazing. Mountain peaks jutted like teeth through the clouds. Mount Everest rose in the distance, towering above the others. Wind whipped snow off the mountaintops.

When they dropped through the clouds, they saw birds swimming gracefully through the air over rocky plains where herds of yak grazed on grassy patches. Sunlight shimmered off the golden roofs of Buddhist shrines scattered like crumbs over the scenery. A canyon snaked through the mountains, like the earth's deep veins. Neither of the twins would admit it, but it was a beautiful sight.

"This is just like the second season of *Million Dollar Mountain Challenge*," Celia said.

"They had to eat bugs," Oliver added.

Celia groaned. "We better not have to eat bugs."

"Like the Thanksgiving before Mom left."

Oliver remembered that night. They had a turkey, like a normal family, but his mother made her favorite recipe from Thailand: roasted centipede and cornbread stuffing with a spicy peanut curry sauce. His stomach, already weary from the airplane food and the fall out of the airplane, felt like it did a backflip. He thought he might *yak* himself.

That Thanksgiving had been a lot of fun. They had played a geography quiz game, naming all the most extreme points on earth (Mount Everest, in front of them, was the highest mountain, and the Tsangpo Gorge, right below them, was the steepest canyon). After the game, they curled up on the couch and watched a movie. They had to watch it on an old film projector. Their mother loved those old projectors. She loved the sounds they made and the antiqueness of it all. She loved how *real* they were. She refused to have their home movies transferred to DVD. She even refused to own a DVD player.

She always said that one day the film reels and the old projectors would be civilization's artifacts for future explorers to discover. They would think it was a kind of ancient magic, how people put little images on film and moved them in front of a light to make them tell stories.

"They are like our shamans," she would say. "They are our mystic storytellers, conjuring visions and images from light and air. How is a projector anything other than magic?" Their mother made watching a movie seem like an important thing to do.

Oliver couldn't remember what the movie was that they watched that night, but his mother laughed the whole way through it, while she snuggled with his father, and they popped fried beetles into each other's mouths (instead of popcorn). Professor Rasmali-Greenberg had come by with some old nautical charts to review, forgetting that it was an American holiday. He ended up watching the movie with the family, and laughing at jokes none of the Navels thought were funny. It was a great night. Too bad his mother had to ruin it all by running off on her adventure just after the New Year. Oliver wiped a tear from his eye.

"Are you okay?" his sister asked.

"Yeah, just that the wind is making my eyes water," he said.

"Yeah . . . me too," she said, and Oliver noticed

that her eyes were red and teary also. "I wonder where we'll land," she added. "They took all of Dad's maps and books."

"At least we still have this," Oliver said, and pulled the scrap of paper with their mother's note and sketches and the ancient Greek writing from their father's pocket. It flapped in the wind. "Let's put it in the backpack. So it doesn't get lost."

"I think that air marshal and that stewardess were working for Sir Edmund," Celia said.

"Really?"

"Yeah, they seemed to know each other and the man next to me who started it all. He was definitely a spy. And they both had matching rings on, rings that made me think of Sir Edmund's emblem. They were different, but they reminded me of it. They were these jeweled keys."

"Would Sir Edmund really want us killed?"

"What do you think?"

Oliver remembered what Sir Edmund had said about their father, and he knew that Sir Edmund would do anything to get what he wanted. That's how he got rich. Their parents always said that discovery was its own reward. Sir Edmund thought reward was its own reward.

"If we don't find these tablets, then he'll win the bet with Dad . . ."

"I don't even want to think about it. If he's willing to throw us out of an airplane to get what he wants, imagine what he'd do if we were his slaves!"

Oliver shuddered at the thought. Celia looked glum.

While adventures that took them away from the television were bad, forced labor for Sir Edmund every vacation until they turned eighteen would be even worse. The bet their father had made for their freedom was totally unfair. And Celia couldn't shake the feeling that they'd fallen right into Sir Edmund's plans. In the library, he had said something about a Council, about his plans for the Navel family. She couldn't make sense of it at all. It was more complicated than trying to pick up a TV show in the middle of the season.

"So." Celia decided to change the subject. Secret Councils and ancient documents were her father's concern, not hers. She was just trying to make sure they got back home alive. "Can we steer this thing?"

Oliver reached up and pulled on one of the

cords attached to the parachute. The raft swung hard to the left and tilted, nearly dumping all three of them over the edge.

"Not without killing ourselves in the process," Oliver said.

"Let's not do that again," Celia said.

"I agree," said her brother, looking toward the ground far below. "I hope landing doesn't kill us anyway."

# 11

# WE DISCUSS
# THE LOCAL NEWS

**AFTER ABOUT FIVE MORE** minutes drifting through the sky, the bottom of the raft started to skim the snowy boulders and jagged trees on the edge of a mountain.

"We're almost down," Oliver said. "I hope we don't get stuck in a—ouch!"

"Are you all right?"

"A tree branch just poked me in the butt," he said as he shifted uncomfortably. They saw their father's limp body jolt. For a second, they thought he was awake, but it was just another branch whacking him from underneath. "Dad's going to have some bruises."

"I hope he's not mad," Celia said.

"He'd be dead if not for us," Oliver said. "And

we nearly died because of him . . . *as usual.* If anyone gets to be mad, it should be us."

Suddenly, with a terrible crunching, cracking, breaking noise, the raft smashed through a sheet of snow, scraped off a boulder and, suddenly rolling and spinning, became like a sled, screaming down the side of the Roof of the World. Colorful birds took flight all around them. A small red panda cocked its head curiously as the bright yellow raft streaked past, trailing its strange parachute like a tail.

"Ahhhh!" both children screamed together. They raced along, the world a blur of white and blue and green. Rocks and bushes smashed into them, knocking their raft around like a pinball.

"Oh, no!" Celia shouted.

"What is it?" Oliver screamed back to her, because his eyes were closed.

"A cliff!"

Oliver opened his eyes and saw that they were about to go over the edge. Their parachute was shredded. All he could think to do as they took to the sky again was grab his father's ankle and scream.

"Ahhhh!" both children yelled as they were yanked brutally backwards.

................................................................

They stopped.

Their parachute had tangled and snagged on a boulder, and the life raft swung to a stop several thousand feet above a raging river in the gorge below. The children were dumped into each other, with their father lying on top of them. The raft made a creaking noise as it settled and swung in the breeze. A bright red bird perched for a moment on their father's foot, screeched and flew off again.

"Are we alive?" Celia wondered, her father's foot smashing into her face.

"I think so," Oliver answered, his face dug into his father's armpit. "It smells like we are."

"Hmmm," Celia added. At this point, the raft was more like a hammock. They were piled on top of each other in a jumble of legs and arms. Celia was looking down toward the forest and the river, while Oliver was twisted upward, looking at the sky and the icy walls on top of the cliff. They hung for a while with the high mountain wind howling against their yellow raft.

"Hey," Oliver asked, forming an idea. "What's below us?"

"A river," Celia said.

"The riverbank could be pretty soft," Oliver

said, remembering Choden Thordup's story about jumping from the window of the monastery.

"So?"

Oliver suggested shoving his father down and then landing on him like a cushion.

"Like Stephen the Yak," he said. "Dad wouldn't mind. He's not even awake."

Celia said no to the idea.

"Daddy's girl," Oliver sneered.

They dangled from the cliff for what felt like hours. They heard a growl in the distance and the calls of strange birds. Below them stretched a dense forest. Above them, the craggy mountain was quilted with patches of white snow. Every few minutes something would creak, and Celia feared it would be the end. But still, they hung. Their father snorted loudly, but didn't wake up.

Above him, Oliver watched a massive tiger creep along the narrow ridge and sniff at the tangle of canvas and plastic that attached them to the cliff. One push from his giant paw and they'd fall over the edge. Oliver had learned all about Tibetan tigers on *Asia's Deadliest Animals Two: CAT-astrophe*.

Tibetan tigers are nearly extinct, he thought.

And they don't normally live at this high altitude. Then again, I don't normally live at this high altitude either.

Only the hungriest tiger would dare come so close to humans. Was it crazy or starving? Or both? Celia and Oliver would make a nice snack, wrapped in yellow plastic and hanging like peanut butter crackers in a vending machine. The tiger didn't move or make a sound. It stayed at the edge, poised. The wind ruffled its orange and black fur, but otherwise, it was as still as a statue.

Celia couldn't see the tiger from where she was. She didn't even know that a tiger was watching them. She was watching the river below them and getting more and more antsy. Hanging upside down for an hour was really boring and really uncomfortable, like going to the opera. Her neck was starting to ache from her father's body smushing her. She really wanted to be at home right now, comfy on the couch watching something about romance or a game show or anything that didn't involve hanging upside down off a cliff with her brother and her unconscious father in the highest place in the world.

Oliver watched the tiger lick its lips. All this

falling from the sky and hanging from trees and giant hungry tigers was growing tiresome, and Oliver was fed up.

"I am fed up," he said. The tiger let out a low growl and didn't take his eyes off of Oliver. "This is so boring."

"I've been looking at the same patch of mist for an hour," Celia complained.

The tiger still didn't move.

"Nothing is happening," Oliver said. "This is like watching a blender commercial."

"Or an awards ceremony."

"Or the local news."

"Ugh," Celia said. "You win. It's like that. Only without the threat of deadly escalators or killer pickle jars."

The tiger moved on, having lost interest in the children.

"I hate this!" Oliver pouted. His sister hated when her brother pouted. He had this way of sticking his chin out and clenching his forehead and it looked like he was going to cry or explode or both. "We should be home on the couch where there aren't any evil flight attendants or deep gorges or giant boring tigers or tall men with machine guns!"

"I know, but stop whining, would you—wait. Tigers?! What? Tall men with what?"

"Up there," Oliver said. "Right above us."

Celia bent her head around to look up and saw that, indeed, there was a very tall man standing on the rock where their raft was caught. He had a machine gun and was pointing it at them.

He was bald and his face was wide, with deep wrinkles. He was quite old, but how old the children could not tell. He wore simple sandals with socks, light pants and a monk's robes. Over his robes, he had a bandolier of bullets, like a cowboy in an old western, except the bullets were long and thin, and clearly intended for the machine gun he was holding. Each bullet was carved with a pattern of symbols. He had a small backpack on his back.

"Dr. Navel?" he shouted down to them in English, much to the children's surprise. "Are you alive?"

"Ummm, we think he is," Oliver yelled back.

"Who are you?" Celia shouted up. Oliver was always too willing to talk to strangers. Celia was far more careful. She wished her brother would let her do the talking.

"My name is Lama Norbu," the man answered,

as if it was the most obvious thing in the world. "And I assume you must be Celia and Oliver."

"Yeah . . ." Oliver said hesitantly.

"And your father?"

"He got knocked out by an air marshal and a stewardess. They threw us out of the plane," Oliver said.

"Shhhh . . ." Celia whispered. "Don't tell him too much. We don't know if we can trust him yet."

"You don't look like a llama," Oliver called up to the old man. Oliver had seen a cartoon about a talking llama, so perhaps, he thought, they could exist. He never thought he'd meet one in the real world.

"No, I suppose I don't," was all the man said in explanation, and then he broke into a wide gleeful smile. "I am glad to see you are alive. I had arranged with your father and Ms. Thordup to pick you up at the airport, and it seems I won't be able to. I apologize. I would, however, be happy to help you now. It is not wise to hang there any longer. There are snakes and insects, and much worse here above the gorge."

"We'd appreciate that," Oliver called back, as Celia shot him daggers with her eyes.

"What?" he whispered. "We need to get up somehow."

Lama Norbu went to work right away. He pulled a rope from the knapsack he had slung over his shoulder, tied it to a tree, and before the kids could count to ten, he was hanging from a rock next to them and tying his rope to their raft.

"Greetings!" he said, smiling like he didn't have a care in the world. He was hanging by one hand over the edge of the cliff. He had a dazzling white smile, and though he was old, he was all muscle. Close up, the children saw that he had a thin wisp of a white mustache and bushy eyebrows. His cheeks were rosy red. "It is a pleasure to meet the children of such eminent explorers. When I arranged to be your father's guide, I was thrilled for the chance to meet the rest of the family."

"Not the rest of the family," Oliver corrected. "Our mother isn't here."

"But in spirit!" said Lama Norbu cheerfully. "In the spirit of adventure, I am sure she is with you!" He laughed loudly.

"Whatever," said Celia.

"Anyway, I am not a llama," the monk explained. The wind howled against the raft. "The llama is a

South American *camelid* growing to about five and a half feet tall and used by the Incan civilization as a pack animal. I am a *lama*, with one *l*. A lama-with-one-*l* is a teacher who has spent lifetimes in study and good deeds. I am also well over six feet tall, and would tower over any llama I came across." He laughed again.

"Oh," the children said warily.

"You two must be very brilliant explorers, just like your parents," the old man added.

"No," both children said in unison.

"Okaaay . . ." said Lama Norbu. He quickly changed the subject. "I dreamed something like this might happen," he said as he scurried back up the cliff using the rope. "The hidden lands have called you to them. *Om mani padme hum!*" He began to hoist the raft up with his rope. He was much stronger than the Navel Twins could have imagined possible for such an old guy. When they reached the top, the man chanted again: "*Om mani padme hum.*"

Oliver and Celia glanced at each other, wondering if the tall man was crazy. A talking llama might make more sense.

"That is a *mantra*," Lama Norbu explained. "A

saying that we often repeat to gain wisdom. Its sounds contain the entire teachings of the Buddha." He smiled. Oliver and Celia were not comforted. He seemed like a total loon.

"So you're a lama, huh?" Oliver said.

"How exactly did you find us here?" asked Celia.

"Things always go wrong in life," he said. "Certainty is an illusion. The odds of finding you here were as good as meeting you at the airport. So I imagined what disaster could befall you, and took a walk into the canyon. Since all space is a creation of the mind, this cliff is the same as the airport. You might as well have been here as anywhere. And perhaps you are!"

He gestured to the landscape, still grinning from ear to ear. Monkeys howled in the distance.

Once they were out of their ruined raft, Lama Norbu shook both of the children's hands with a smile. He bent down to their level and looked them right in the eyes in a way that made them feel respected. Though he was tall, he didn't seem to look down on them.

"Grhumgughhhphhh . . ." said Dr. Navel as he started to wake up. After a moment of rocking his head back and forth and groaning, his eyes snapped open and he sat bolt upright. *"Unhand my children!"* he shouted.

"It's okay, Dad. We're safe. We're on the ground," said Celia. "Sort of."

"We met Lama Norbu," said Oliver. "He says he's not a llama."

"Oh." Dr. Navel looked around and rubbed the back of his neck where a branch had whacked him. There was a bump on his forehead where the air marshal hit him. He pushed his glasses up on his nose and sprang to his feet, showing no confusion about where he was or how he got there. He smiled his winning smile, as if nothing at all out of the ordinary had happened. Then he fell down again.

Lama Norbu came over and helped the explorer to his feet once more.

"Greetings, Lama Norbu. So nice to finally meet you." Dr. Navel pulled a long white silk scarf from under his shirt and presented it to the old man, bowing his head low. His children watched him curiously, but the old man did not seem surprised.

"Greetings, Ogden," said Lama Norbu, using their father's first name, which almost no one ever did. He accepted the scarf graciously and hung it around his neck under his cloak.

"Well, my friends, shall we be on our way, then?" their father said. He wiped his hands on his pants and looked up and down the cliff. "Lama Norbu, lead the way, sir!"

"But there's no path," Celia pointed out. "We're on the edge of a cliff."

"There is always a path," explained Lama Norbu. "If your mind is open, you will find there is always a path out of your troubles. And in the quest for Shangri-La there are many paths . . . and many troubles." He laughed at his little joke, and then pointed in front of him. Sure enough, there was a narrow path along the edge of the cliff, leading down into the forest below. "The path provided is not always the easiest," he explained. "But it is always what is needed. We are meant to descend into the valley, it seems."

He slung his gun onto his back and started to walk down.

"What about going to see the protector-spirit, Dorjee Drakden?" Dr. Navel asked. "Won't we need his blessing?"

"The path tells us to go down, so we go down,"

the lama replied quickly. "Perhaps the spirit will find us, perhaps not. And truthfully," he said, lowering his voice to a near whisper, and losing his smile for the first time, "I do not know if we can trust the protector anymore. He has grown unpredictable. Times are dangerous."

For a moment Celia thought she saw a guilty look slide across Lama Norbu's face, but the moment passed and his face snapped back into a smile. He turned and continued down the path, singing a little tune. Dr. Navel shrugged and followed close behind.

"Oh, children," he said, turning over his shoulder to look at the twins. "Stay close so you don't fall or get dragged off by any demons. And watch out for the *Dugmas*—Poison Witches can be tricky. And also thanks for"—he pointed up at the sky—"you know, whatever you did. Well done!" He smiled broadly, as if this whole situation was just the most fun he'd ever had, which in his mind it may have been. Then he turned and continued after the old monk scrambling down the side of the canyon.

Oliver and Celia looked at each other in disbelief. Was that really all they got from their dad after saving his life? Celia scooped up their backpack, threw it onto her back and sighed. Oliver turned to go first, like always. Reluctantly, they followed their father down, toward the sound of howling monkeys and dangers they wouldn't even want to see on television.

# 12

# WE LEARN ABOUT LAMAS AND LEOPARDS AND LIFE ITSELF

**THE NAVELS FOLLOWED** Lama Norbu down the narrow path for what felt like hours, tripping over gnarly rocks and bushes. Oliver and Celia were tired from traveling all night and most of a day, falling out of an airplane, hanging from the edge of a cliff, being rescued by a machine-gun-toting lama, and hiking into the deepest canyon in the world. They usually found Mr. Busick's gym class exhausting.

A scorpion scurried up a rock face as they passed, and two dark black birds chirped at them, flashing their wings to show the bright feathers on the underside, brilliant rainbows of color that seemed to glow against the rest of their ink-black bodies.

"There's nothing to watch," Oliver whined as he watched the birds take off into the sky.

"Nothing worth watching, anyway," Celia clarified for her brother, who rolled his eyes at her. She really liked being right.

Their father tried to keep them entertained.

"Look at that," he said, pointing to a giant tree that looked like the thousands of other giant trees around them. "That tree right there is one of the last of the great Asian sequoias."

"Great," the children groaned. "Trees. Whoopee."

"And that bush there sprouts berries whose juice is poisonous to every creature on earth except one kind of beetle. And that beetle doesn't even live on this continent. There's no explanation for it! Isn't it wonderful?"

"Sure," the kids said flatly.

"Shangri-La is a hidden land," added Lama Norbu, trying to spark the twins' interest and seeing that their father's science wasn't working. "Many explorers believe it does not even exist, while many others have been lost searching for it. It will be a perilous journey to try to find it. There are ancient maps created by wise men, but no one knows how to read them."

"Then how do you know where we're going?" Celia said, nervous that they themselves were going to get lost. Maybe this is where their mother got lost.

"Oh, I lived in this valley many lifetimes ago," Lama Norbu replied calmly. "I have been a monkey howling from these trees and a fish swimming in these raging rivers. These hidden lands are drawn like a map in my soul."

Oliver and Celia looked at each other with their eyebrows raised. The lama talked exactly like wise men on television shows, almost like he had a script that he didn't really understand himself. Dr. Navel nodded as if it all made total sense, as if it was perfectly rational to have a map in your soul and to use it to get around.

"Wonderful!" he said.

Of course, Dr. Navel, like fathers everywhere, hated to ask for directions and probably wished he had a map of *everywhere* written in his soul so he wouldn't have to pull into a gas station looking sheepish ever again.

"Okay, that's it," Oliver finally said and stopped walking. He had had enough weird for one day. "How could you have been a monkey and a fish and, you know, yourself? How could you have been around for many lifetimes? Are you, like, a vampire?"

"Oh, no." Lama Norbu laughed, slapping his knees and leaning against a tall tree. "A vampire! What a strange idea! No, I am not, nor have I ever been a vampire. Nor will I ever be, I pray. Their skin is like fire to the touch, their necks are long and thin, their bellies hang to their toes, and they groan with thirst for thousands of years. I pray you never meet one."

"That's not how vampires are at all," Celia objected. "They have alabaster skin and eyes like the sea during a storm. They have dark passions and wander the earth looking for love."

"It would be quite impossible to fall in love with a real vampire," Lama Norbu said and chuckled. "They are incapable of even speaking, and love nothing but misery."

"Okay, you're not a vampire," interrupted Oliver, because he knew how his sister felt about vampires and he didn't want to see her punch the old lama in the nose. She had a crush on Corey Brandt, who played the teenage vampire on *Sunset High*, which was canceled after the first season. It broke her heart, especially when it was replaced with *Agent Zero*. She didn't care that it had the exact same actor. She had a thing for vampires. "So how were you a monkey?"

"A vampire would never take the form of a monkey," Celia muttered under her breath so only her brother heard her.

"Reincarnation," Lama Norbu said. "The cycle of death and rebirth."

"I see," said Oliver, though he didn't see.

"We monks believe that all living things are born and die and are reborn over and over again, and how we are reborn depends upon what we do while we are alive. We will continue to return to earth again and again, rising and falling— sometimes a beetle, sometimes a god, but always returning until we become enlightened and are set free."

"So it's like reruns," said Oliver.

Lama Norbu just furrowed his brow. He knew a lot about life and death and eternity, but nothing about television. "It is karma," he said. "If you do evil in life, you might be reborn a demon, but if you do great good deeds, you might be reborn as a great ruler, even a god."

Celia liked the idea of being reborn as a god. She'd be all-powerful. Then she wouldn't have to go on these crazy adventures and could just sit on a throne and watch the world like it was a TV show. And she could watch what *she* wanted. Gods didn't have to let their twin brothers watch *The World's Greatest Animal Chases Three*. It seemed too good to be true.

"Dad, do you really believe in all this stuff?" Celia asked her father. "Rebirth, and gods and oracles and hidden lands with all the wisdom of the world hidden there? I mean, it can't be real."

"I learned long ago that the line between real and unreal is quite blurry," Dr. Navel said. "Think about your television. If you showed it to a group of people who lived their whole lives in little huts in this valley, they would think it was magic. Just like you think it's crazy that there can be reincarnation and oracles and hidden lands, other people might think it's crazy that humans have walked on the moon or that we watch little glowing boxes for hours and hours and hours."

"So if Shangri-La is real, how are we supposed to find it?" Celia said. "I want to get to it as quickly as possible and get home. All the good summer shows start next week." She pulled out their mother's note and handed it to her dad.

Dr. Navel just shook his head and looked down at the note. "Her writing's not easy to read: 'November fourth, little time left; they are close behind me, letting me search for the missing pages until they strike. I'm closer now than I've imagined. No one thought the Great Library might be in Shangri-La. Only the shamans' eyes can tell the way from here.' " He looked up at Lama Norbu. "What shamans do you think she meant?"

"There are many shamans in this valley," Lama Norbu said. "Some good. Some evil. Her clue isn't very helpful, I'm afraid."

"So where do we find some of them?" Oliver asked. Celia couldn't believe that they were actually doing this. Oliver secretly liked the idea of meeting a shaman, but he didn't want to let his sister know. She'd think he was becoming an explorer. He'd seen a show about shamans once, and thought they were cool. He imagined them with bones through their noses dancing around fires in front of camera crews.

"That's hard to say," Lama Norbu answered. "Anyone could be a shaman. A shaman is just someone who can show people things they cannot see themselves."

"So I could be a shaman," Celia said. "I can see that we should be at home right now instead of wandering around in some valley on the other side of the world!"

"Oh, to be a shaman takes great powers of meditation," Lama Norbu answered her. "You must clear your mind and sit very still and focus. It can take hours, days, years, even lifetimes of sitting and meditating to see the truth. Life is filled with many dangers and distractions to keep you from this path."

"Like the abominable snowman?" asked Oliver.

Lama Norbu smiled. "No, the yeti, or as you call him, the abominable snowman, is just a legend. The real dangers are in your mind. They are your illusions and your selfishness."

"So that yeti right there is an illusion?" Oliver said, pointing at the giant white creature that stood on its hind legs in front of them. It looked like a cross between a polar bear and a person. Its teeth were the size of a man's fingers and were stained with dried blood. Everyone turned toward it and it roared. Birds took flight and leaves shook. The forest grew still and silent with fear.

"No," Lama Norbu said, slowly moving for his gun. "I fear that creature is very real and wishes to send us to our next rebirth sooner than we would like."

# 13

# WE BLAST
# SOME BLESSINGS
# THROUGH THE AIR

**THE CREATURE LOWERED** down to all fours and snarled and scratched deep grooves into the ground with its long black claws.

"No one move," Lama Norbu whispered. "A creature like this would never reveal herself to humans. She must be desperate and therefore very dangerous."

"She?" Celia said.

"Yes," he answered. "In the stories I have heard, the females are much larger than the males. They are also more aggressive."

"Amazing!" Dr. Navel exclaimed. He dropped their mother's note on the ground. He was entranced. The excitement of the discovery washed away any fear he felt, and he stepped closer to get a better look at the furry giant. Fear, he always said, was the most boring of the emotions. Oliver and Celia found it pretty useful. They jumped backwards.

"Dad . . ." both of them warned. Their father cocked his head to the side like a curious puppy while the creature's black marble eyes stared back at him.

"Ogden, I must warn you that . . ." Lama Norbu began, but before he could finish the monster had sprung from where it crouched to a boulder above Dr. Navel and, in one swipe of her giant paw, sent the curious adventurer hurtling through the air off the side of the mountain.

"Dad!" Celia shouted. Lama Norbu spun the gun off his back but tripped over a rock as he stepped forward. Oliver, moving with speed he didn't know he had, snatched the gun from the ground and waved it toward the creature.

"Back up!" he yelled, because he didn't know what else to yell. He had never held a gun before, nor had he ever yelled at a monster. He waved the gun at the monster again, just to make sure his point was clear.

The yeti cocked its head curiously at Oliver, just like his father had cocked his head curiously at the yeti.

"Hey," Oliver called out. "Shoo!"

"Shoo?" Celia shouted. "Shoo??"

"I don't know! What should I yell?" Oliver called back.

"Try shouting!"

"Aaaaargh!" Oliver shouted, and waved the gun over his head like it was a spear.

The monster roared and took a huge swipe at Oliver with her giant paws. He dove out of the way.

"That didn't work!" he yelled. The monster swiped again and snagged the edge of Oliver's shirt as he jumped backward.

Oliver dove right and left, trying to dodge the giant yeti. When it lunged at Oliver again, he jumped up and caught onto its back. He saw it was wearing a collar and he held on to it for dear life.

"Throw me the rifle!" Lama Norbu called out.

Oliver tossed the rifle toward Lama Norbu, so he could hold on with both hands, though he missed the throw by several feet, and Lama Norbu had to go scrambling after the gun. The yeti tried to get Oliver off her back by leaping and spinning.

Oliver rode the monster like a cowboy riding a bull.

"Ahhhh!" he shouted, and actually wished that all he had to deal with right now were lizard bites. The yeti stopped thrashing and started to charge backward toward the wall of rock behind them. She wanted to slam Oliver against it and crush him. He unbuckled the collar and dove off the yeti, just as Lama Norbu reached the gun. The creature turned and charged right at the monk, swiping the gun out of his hands. It flew through the air and Celia caught it.

"I don't know what to do!" she yelled, and tossed the gun to her brother, like a hot potato, while Lama Norbu ran in circles, chased by the angry yeti. Oliver didn't have time to think or to aim. He'd seen enough cowboy movies to know what to do. He pointed the gun at the monster and closed his eyes and squeezed the trigger.

"Ahhhhhhhh!!!!" he yelled as the gun kicked and bucked in his hand, nearly knocking him over. The gun's recoil felt like a punch in the arm from a bear. He opened his eyes to see what he'd done, and prayed he hadn't accidentally shot his sister or Lama Norbu.

The yeti stood upright and looked back at Oliver. She turned toward him, puzzled. He raised the gun again, but didn't really know if he had the strength to fire it.

"Sorry," he muttered, and knew he would never be much of a hunter. He didn't have the aim, the arms or the stomach for it.

The yeti roared and pounded her chest like a gorilla, and then took one big leap, effortlessly jumping over Oliver and bounding up from boulder to boulder.

In seconds the creature was gone into the mist, and only the echo of its roar lingered in the air.

The twins ran to the edge of the cliff and peered over the side. They saw their father hanging by one hand from a tangle of roots. The ground was thousands of feet below him. He smiled up at his children.

"Well, that was unexpected," he said. His face was a little bruised and his glasses cracked, but his good mood was unflappable. "That must be the creature that the Royal Geographical Society claimed to have discovered in nineteen twenty-one! The Wild Man of the Snows! They called it the yeti, which is probably a mispronunciation of the Tibetan words for 'man' and 'bear.' Amazing! I can't say it looked much like a man, but—"

"Excuse me, Doctor, but would you like us to lift you up?" Lama Norbu interrupted as he took the rifle from Oliver's shaking hands. Dr. Navel had gotten so excited by his ideas about the yeti that he'd forgotten he was hanging off the edge of a cliff.

"That would be appreciated, thank you," he replied, smiling.

For the second time that day, Lama Norbu scurried down the side of the cliff to rescue Dr. Navel. This time the kids watched from above and talked while Lama Norbu hoisted.

"So that was a yeti," Oliver said.

"I guess so," Celia answered.

"I just shot at the abominable snowman!"

"Snow*woman*, and yeah, I guess you did."

"Do you think I hurt her?"

"It didn't look like you hit her at all. You don't have very good aim."

"Well, I never shot at a mythical creature before, so excuse me. I didn't see you racing to the rescue."

"You're a real Agent Zero," Celia said sarcastically, but Oliver took it as a pretty huge compliment. He stood a little taller and smiled.

"Remember the special we saw, *Monsters—Myth or Reality: The Expert Files*?" Celia asked.

"Yeah."

"And you couldn't sleep for a week because you thought there was a yeti under your bed."

"I did not think there was a yeti under my bed," Oliver said, his pride deflating like a day-old birthday balloon.

"You did too," his sister said.

"Not a yeti. A basilisk, which is a kind of snake demon. That's totally different from a yeti."

"Well, that's not the point anyway."

"What is the point then?"

"Remember what Sir Edmund said about bigfoot, and the basilisk and . . ."

"The yeti." Oliver's eyes grew wide. "Ycah, he said he had them in his zoo. He was talking about it at that banquet."

"Right."

The twins knew that Sir Edmund collected rare creatures the way some people collect stamps or playing cards or action figures. Sometimes he hunted them and hung their stuffed heads on his wall, sometimes he sold them, and sometimes he kept them in his zoo. His hobby was a lot more dangerous than collecting playing cards.

"He could easily have dropped that yeti in front of us, ready to attack," Celia said.

"I think so too," Oliver said, and held up the collar. It had a symbol engraved on it: a scroll locked in chains.

"Which means we must be on the right track to finding those tablets," said Celia.

"We better get cable if we survive this."

"Yeah," she answered.

"At least we have Lama Norbu and his gun for protection."

"Not really, children, I am sorry," Lama Norbu said, suddenly standing beside them.

"What?"

"The gun is not real," he said. "That is why you did not hit the creature when you shot at it, Oliver. We Buddhists do not believe in violence, so a real gun, whose only purpose is to kill, would be unthinkable. This weapon fires blessings, loud ones."

He smiled and showed them his "bullets." Each one was carved with elaborate symbols and images of angry-looking Buddhas sitting on lotus flowers.

"The symbols represent the mantra I told you about, *om mani padme hum*, and the pictures are of the wrathful Buddha, who is angry at the suffering of the world and destroys pain and death with his anger. The bullets do not fire, they just sound like it, like fireworks, so that even as I seem violent, I am actually firing blessings into the sky, showering my enemies with wisdom and kindness."

"So I blessed that monster?" Oliver said with relief.

"Exactly," Lama Norbu said. "You did a double good deed by saving our lives and blessing the yeti."

"So, if it hadn't been afraid of the exploding blessings . . ." Celia wondered.

"We would surely have all been eaten." Lama Norbu smiled. "That is why we must find a place to rest for the night. We cannot wander the canyon after dark."

"Because of other monsters?" asked Oliver, nervous. He was sure Sir Edmund had worse than the abominable snowman planned for them.

"Not monsters," said Lama Norbu. "We who are

pure of heart have nothing to fear from the monsters of the hidden lands. *People* present much more of a problem for us. There are bandits in these forests."

"Bandits!" cried Celia. Bandits had hijacked the plane on *Love at 30,000 Feet,* and she never forgot the way they shouted and threatened to throw the Duchess in Business Class out of the window. Now that Celia herself had fallen out of an airplane, she knew that it was not the most pleasant experience. "We should definitely not walk after dark," she agreed.

She picked their mother's note up off the ground and shoved it into their backpack. Their father was clearly too excited to carry their only clue. Who knew when he'd go chasing after some dangerous animal again?

"Where should we camp?" Dr. Navel asked. "A cave? A lean-to?" He sounded very excited about a cave or a lean-to. He loved sleeping in uncomfortable places. We should not be surprised to learn that Celia and Oliver did not share his excitement.

"How about down there?" Lama Norbu said, pointing to the slope just below them.

There was a circle of small round huts less than two hundred yards away. A large fire burned in the center of the circle, and a group of women were squatting around it.

There were several unusual things about this camp, but Celia only noticed one: the largest hut had a satellite dish attached to its roof, and wires snaked from it into the little building. With a satellite dish, you could pick up channels from all over the world.

"This seems like a good place to camp," Celia said.

"This might not be the worst trip of our lives after all." Oliver smiled. "I wonder if they get the Reality Network?"

"And the Soap Channel," Celia added. Dr. Navel just shook his head at his children and sighed, and they all made their way carefully down the slope toward the strange camp.

# 14

# WE HAVE A TV DINNER

**THEY WERE MET** by a group of smiling Tibetan women wearing colorful clothes and handmade jewelry. The women were not young, but they didn't look old either. They looked, strangely, *ageless*. All of them, however, had dirty teeth, and all of their teeth had been filed down to sharp points.

Lama Norbu called out to them in his language, and the women answered with smiles and bows.

"They welcome us to their camp," he explained. "They are just preparing dinner and would be honored if we would stay the night. We will be safe here."

"Please, come in," one of the women said in English. She had a turquoise headband encrusted with shining stones and heavy rings on her fingers. "You are very welcome here. We receive many travelers and it would be our pleasure to be your hosts."

The other women nodded and gestured toward some logs that were spread around the fire. They rushed to cover each log with a thick animal fur so it would be a more comfortable seat. Two of them ran off to continue cooking, while the others ushered the family to the logs to rest their tired feet. They took hospitality very seriously.

"You are American?" asked the one with the headband, who appeared to be their leader.

"We are citizens of the world," Dr. Navel answered, as he always answered that question when someone asked. He didn't like to be defined by borders.

"Yes," Celia said, because she wanted to hurry the conversation along and get to watching the satellite TV. Her father shot her an annoyed look.

"Yankee Doodle dandy!" one of the other women sang, laughing. "Old McDonald had a farm!"

"She speaks no English," the woman with the headband explained. "But she knows many songs."

"Can't buy me lo-ove," she sang, smiling and nodding. "The Beatles!"

"I do hope you will join us for a meal," the other one said, ignoring the woman who kept singing pieces of Beatles songs.

"I am fasting while we look for Shangri-La," Lama Norbu said to the Navels. "But please, enjoy this food. These women are from the Bön sect, the oldest religion in Tibet, and you could learn much from them. I will seek out a quiet area to meditate, now that we have found a safe resting place for the night."

With that he bowed politely and wandered off past the camp and into the thick brush of the forest.

"He is a strange man, this monk," the woman with the headband said.

"He's a lama," Oliver said. "Not a llama."

"I see," the woman answered quizzically.

"Thank you for having us," Dr. Navel said as he settled onto a log. "I am very eager to learn about your culture."

"Oh," said the woman. "We are just simple women who have spent our lives in this canyon.

Our only knowledge of the world comes from that television and from the pilgrims who pass this way. We are not great explorers like you."

Celia and Oliver shifted anxiously on their feet. They wanted to get to the television already. They kept glancing at the hut with the satellite dish.

"I am sure you know a great deal more than you think," Dr. Navel said.

"Dad," Celia whispered. "Can we please go watch the television? Pretty please?" She made her sweetest puppy-dog face.

"This is a once-in-a-lifetime opportunity. You can hear about the ancient ways of the Bön—did you know that they place their dead on tall towers of stone and let the vultures eat the corpses instead of burying them?"

"That's disgusting," said Oliver.

"That's not disgusting, Oliver. It's called sky burial. Their culture represents an entirely different way of imagining the world than you and I have. Remember what I said about—"

"Yes, yes . . . television is magic . . . wonders of the world . . . blah blah blah . . . we get it. But we walked all day and we got thrown out of a plane and we saved your life," Celia said.

"Twice," added Oliver, not wanting them to forget his heroics with the rifle that fired blessings.

"We shouldn't have to learn about new cultures too." Celia felt the need to make their position very clear to their father.

"The children are welcome to rest in front of the television," the woman with the headband said. "We receive many channels they might enjoy." She winked at them.

"All right," Dr. Navel sighed. "Go on."

The twins rushed off to the hut while their father began asking excited questions about myths and legends and human sacrifice. The woman with the headband, in spite of what she had said, knew quite a lot about all of those things, especially the last one.

"The shinbone's connected to the knee bone," sang the musical woman.

Inside the hut, there was another log spread with furs facing the television, and steaming hot bowls of food were set beside it, as if the children were expected.

"Nice women," Oliver said. "They even made us snacks."

The bowls were filled with what looked like curdled milk, all clumpy and grayish, with yellowish chunks of butter floating around and thick mounds of crushed barley. Each bowl had one lump of blackened meat sitting in it, the fat still sizzling. It smelled like chili peppers, leather and wet dog.

"What is that?" Celia wondered.

"It's yak," Oliver said, his face turning green.

"How do you know?" Celia asked nervously, not really wanting to hear the answer.

"Because . . ." Oliver pointed at the wall, where a pile of fur and bones was topped by a giant skull with dark black horns: a slaughtered yak.

Both children turned quickly and tried to put the frightening image from their minds. They thought for a second about running back outside, but out there the women would insist on watching them eat; that much they knew about hospitality. Inside with the yak skeleton they at least had privacy and, of course, television. Oliver grabbed the bowls of food and carefully dumped the lumpy steaming contents behind the pile of bones.

"Sorry," he said, though the creature was long past hearing any apologies for becoming dinner.

While her brother disposed of the "meal," Celia flipped on the old television. It lit up with a static hum.

Outside, they heard their father's voice praising the delicious food.

"Yak butter and barley flour, is it?" he fawned. "It tastes just like my wife used to make before we were married! And you say you make offerings of this to the protector-spirits in the valley? Who are they? Are they violent gods? Helpful?"

They heard the women laughing.

The children looked nervously at each other, but didn't say a word. The screen glowed with fuzzy snow and static. Oliver pulled the cheese puffs out of their backpack for a snack and Celia started turning the tuner. Both children held their breaths in anticipation. The last time they had watched TV was on the airplane, and that had been quite rudely interrupted by Sir Edmund's henchman trying to kill them. This time, deep in the valley on the path to Shangri-La, under the silent gaze of a yak's carcass, they hoped they would finally have some peace and quiet—and some decent entertainment.

When the picture came into focus, Celia shouted

with glee, but Oliver's heart sank into his dirty sneakers.

*"Love at 30,000 Feet!"* she squealed as the theme song played over images of sunsets, jet engines and kissing.

"Oh, no," Oliver groaned.

# 15

# WE WONDER WHY THE LAMA SPEAKS FRANKLY

**ON A BOULDER JUTTING** out into the valley below the camp, Lama Norbu stood with his head bowed, but he was not meditating. His mind was far from peaceful, and the words he muttered scared the birds from their perches. He was angry at the glowing device in his hand, and he whacked it with his palm.

"Come on, you lousy phone!" he cursed. "Get some reception already! What good is a smartphone without any stinking reception?" He smacked the small phone against the side of a tree and it made a series of unhappy beeps, but still didn't dial the number he wanted. "No, I don't want to play Scrabble! I want to make a call!!" he growled at it, and whacked it again. "Aaargh!!"

"That is not a very peace-loving thing to do," a

voice spoke from the darkness behind him. "In fact, I have never in my life met a monk whose meditation involved cursing at a phone."

Sir Edmund stepped from the darkness with a smile on his face. He wore a khaki explorer's outfit with dozens of pockets and a little pith helmet, like something out of an old movie. He strolled over to Lama Norbu like it was perfectly natural for him to be taking a late night walk in the Tsangpo Gorge.

"You," was all Lama Norbu said as he moved his hand toward his rifle.

"Don't bother," said Sir Edmund. "I am not alone and, though you cannot see them, you are surrounded."

"What do you want then? To finish what your abominable snowman could not?"

"Snow*woman*," Sir Edmund said, and laughed. "Anyway, the yeti was just a test. I knew a wise monk like yourself could handle it."

"It nearly killed Dr. Navel."

"They do get rather aggressive when you take their children away," he said. "She's one of the most vicious monsters in my zoo these days."

"You are the monster, Edmund."

Sir Edmund shrugged and looked out over the dark valley, and up to the canopy of stars. It was a beautiful sight, but he didn't seem to be enjoying it.

"Let's cut out the nonsense, shall we?" said Sir Edmund. "We are all impressed that you found the Navels before us. But we had a deal. The Council wants them and you are supposed to bring them to me. You should not have gone off on your own."

"The Council keeps too many secrets."

"The Council has a higher purpose."

"This is also about revenge," Lama Norbu added. He stood even taller and suddenly appeared many years younger than he had appeared moments before. He didn't really look like Lama Norbu at all.

"You are so angry at the Navels you would dare defy us? What would your partner say after we went to all the trouble to arrange this?"

"We both feel the same. After what that Navel woman cost us in the Gobi Desert . . . our price has doubled."

"You are hardly in a position to negotiate. I do wonder what would happen," Sir Edmund chuckled, "if Dr. Navel were to find who you *really* are. Or if the Explorers Club were to learn what had really become of you, the long-lost Frank Pfeffer, discoverer of the Jade Toothpicks."

"You want to blackmail us?"

"I want you to stick to the agreement. If not, you and your partner will be unmasked and, I promise you, destroyed. We had a deal and you will not break that deal."

"Your threats don't frighten me."

"You may have learned the transformative arts from the Hyena People of Gondar, and you have done an admirable job disguising yourself, for such a freakishly tall man, but the truth has a way of shining through. I wonder if I can get Internet access here. Maybe I should update my blog. Does your phone take pictures?" He chuckled. "They make the most remarkable gadgets these days, don't they?"

"You don't have a blog."

"I could start one just for you."

"You are despicable."

"I think the same could be said of you, Frank— I'm sorry, *Lama Norbu*," Sir Edmund sneered. "You don't really have any choice. We'll get what we want whether you help us or not. Our new friends are taking care of that." He turned and walked back into the shadows, murmuring a song as he went. "The ants go marching two by two, hurrah, hurrah!"

Lama Norbu, who wasn't really a monk at all, listened as Sir Edmund's voice faded and then kept listening to the darkness to be sure he was alone once more. He smacked his phone with more urgency this time, and at last, his call got through.

"It's me, Frank," he said into the phone. "The Council found us. I'll have to move quickly now. The tablets will be ours!"

He hung up and sighed into the night.

"And we will have our revenge," he said to no one in particular. He hid the phone back inside his cloak. With a shake of his shoulders he resumed his calm and friendly pose, practicing the monk's smile.

# 16

# WE SEE A BRAND-NEW RERUN

**OLIVER AND CELIA SAT BUG-EYED** in front of the television, stuffing cheese puffs into their mouths. Their faces were blank, their minds even blanker. Nothing existed for them but *Love at 30,000 Feet*. Even Oliver had overcome his resistance to all the kissing and was entranced. The children watched and were happy.

Of course, they didn't understand a word.

The show was dubbed over in Chinese, so that when the actors' mouths moved to make the English words, Chinese words came out. Subtitles ran at the bottom of the screen that indicated what the actors were saying, but the subtitles were in Tibetan, so even reading them was no help. They couldn't tell that *Nga kayrâng-la gawpo yö* meant "I love you" or that *Há la gyuk! Ngempa-po khyö!* meant "Get away, you rogues!" but they could figure out what was going on by facial expressions and lip-reading and how the people moved or shouted at each other. It helped that they had seen every episode.

In this episode, the captain was arguing with his copilot about something. He kept pointing toward the fuel gauge. The copilot pressed a lot of buttons and the plane jerked in all directions. Passengers shouted, and the stewardess said calming things to them, trying to maintain her balance. The actress playing her had bright white teeth and smiled widely in a familiar way, but she wasn't very comforting. She also wasn't very steady on her feet. She fell right into the lap of a man in a shiny birthday clown costume with a bright red nose. He said something to her that made her laugh. He said something else and she slapped him.

Back in the cockpit, the captain regained control of the airplane and everyone cheered. Then he looked at his copilot and said something very serious. His face was pale, his eyes like steel. A tear trickled down the copilot's cheek.

"Captain Sinclair is about to ask the Duchess

in Business Class to tango!" Celia exclaimed. It was her favorite moment in the whole series. She had made Oliver watch this episode at least ten times. She had wanted to watch it again the night their father dragged them to the Ceremony of Discovery.

"I thought this was the one where Captain Sinclair falls unconscious and the traveling birthday clown has to land the plane," Oliver said.

"That wasn't even in this season. Just watch."

"I'm pretty sure Captain Sinclair's about to fall over. You can tell when someone is going to faint on television. They get all pale and wobbly."

"That's romance. He's in love."

"Looks pale and wobbly to me."

"That's what love looks like."

"If you say so."

"Shhh, just watch," Celia hissed.

They watched as Captain Sinclair rose, pale and wobbly, to his feet. He left the cockpit, holding on to the backs of the big leather seats to steady himself as he marched down the aisle. Passengers gazed at him with awe. His uniform was crisp and blue.

When he reached her seat, the captain extended

his hand to the duchess and helped her to stand. He said something to her, and she smiled. His eyes looked glassy and his legs swayed. He didn't fall over, though. And he didn't ask the duchess to tango, either. He pointed her toward the bathroom. Then he went to the stewardess and said *Nga kayrâng-la gawpo yö*, which of course the twins still didn't know meant "I love you," but they did know what it meant when he got down on one knee and proposed to the stewardess with a diamond ring.

"Hey!" The twins said in unison. The twins knew that that wasn't supposed to happen. Oliver and Celia were quite certain that reruns didn't change when you watched them again.

The stewardess broke down in tears and her lips clearly said "Yes, I will. Yes!" even though her voice said something in Chinese and the screen said *Nga kayrâng-la gawpo yö*, which by now the twins guessed meant "I love you."

The show was completely different than they remembered it. And if there was one thing they were sure of, it was how their shows were supposed to go.

"I've never seen this episode," Celia muttered. "Maybe they get different seasons of it here."

Oliver suddenly remembered the yak that came to him in a dream on the airplane. "You will have to remember enduring Love if you want to escape a terrible fate," it had said. *Enduring Love . . .* it must have meant he would have to remember *enduring* that marathon of *Love at 30,000 Feet* that his sister had made him watch. He thought back to that weekend when they watched fifty-two hours of this silly soap opera, only pausing to nap and to go to the bathroom. Their father was away in Bhutan at the time, otherwise he never would have let them spend so long eating junk food in front of the television. Oliver thought as hard as he could through the story of the show, through all those seasons.

"This never happened," he said. He looked closer at the screen. That stewardess *did* look familiar, but not because they had ever seen her on the show before. She was the stewardess from their flight! On her jacket, she wore a gold pin with a tiny key on it. "Do you recognize that symbol?" Oliver asked.

"Yes!" Celia gasped. "That's the symbol from

the tunnel at the Explorers Club and it's what the air marshal and the man in the shiny suit had on their rings when they threw us out of the plane!"

"And I think that birthday clown looks awfully familiar."

"His suit is really shiny . . ."

"There's something else," Oliver observed, terrified. It was his turn to get all pale and wobbly.

"What is it?" his sister asked, alarmed.

"The TV's not even plugged in."

The children looked at the flashing images on the television and then to the limp cord resting on the dirt floor.

The flicker of the TV set cast crazy dancing shadows across the skeleton of the yak in the corner, and the strange dubbed laughter of the smiling stewardess filled them with dread. They remembered the warnings of Choden Thordup and of Lama Norbu, and they both had the same thought at the same time.

"The Poison Witches!"

# 17

# WE DARE A DEAL

**THE CHILDREN RUSHED** from the hut into the night and raced toward the campfire. Their father sat on a log with a pile of empty wooden dinner bowls next to him, and the women sat on other logs around him. He was entertaining them with a story.

"So there we were," he said, "in a cave of white marble beneath the ancient palace at Persepolis. And the staff of the Emperor Cyrus sat on a pedestal in front of us, shining with a mysterious light. I was about to touch it, when my wife pointed up. I followed her gaze and saw that the ceiling was entirely covered in bats. Thousands, tens of thousands of bats. And they were waking up."

The women laughed and gasped. Dr. Navel loved the attention. Oliver and Celia never cared that much for their father's bat stories. They preferred watching the show *Bat Stories* on Saturday morning cartoons.

"Well, my wife said, 'Maybe they'll go back to sleep if we sing to them.' So suddenly, she starts singing this song we used to put Oliver and Celia to bed. And wouldn't you know it—"

"Dad!" the children yelled as they approached. Their father looked up, startled. He was not used to seeing his children run.

"Oliver! Celia!" He smiled. "I was just talking about you."

"These . . . these . . ." Oliver panted.

"These are the Poison Witches!" Celia shouted. The women around the circle gasped.

"Children," Dr. Navel said, his face immediately turning angry. "That is a very, very offensive thing to say. The *Dugmas* are some of the most hated and feared creatures in this land, and it is completely inappropriate to call our hosts such a thing."

"Your children have quite the imagination," the woman with the turquoise headband said, though she was not laughing.

"Not usually," Dr. Navel replied, slightly puzzled. He turned to the children. "Why would you say such a thing?"

"Because," Celia started, "Captain Sinclair should have proposed to the Duchess in Business Class, not the stewardess."

"And the yak on the tiny airplane screen warned me too," Oliver added.

Dr. Navel looked at his children a moment, considering what they were telling him. The fire crackled and hissed and insects buzzed in the darkness beyond.

"Television does not have all the answers," he said at last. "I have spent time with these women, and I assure you that they are lovely hosts and have no intention of poisoning us to steal our souls. Now, if you would please allow me to finish my story, I was just getting to the part where your mother—"

And then their father went pale and wobbly and fell flat on his face on the ground.

"Well, this is not at all how it was supposed to happen," the woman with the headband said. She was clearly their leader.

"It was supposed to be the children who took the poison," another complained.

"Maybe Dr. Navel was tired from all the travel?" another suggested. "What's that called? Jet lag?"

"It's not jet lag," the leader said.

"It could be jet lag. You don't know."

"Did you poison his stew?"

"Maybe."

"You weren't supposed to poison his stew."

"I couldn't remember whose stew to poison, so I poisoned all the stews."

"That wasn't the plan at all!" The witch walked over to Dr. Navel and lifted his hand up, then dropped it again. "You put enough poison in his stew to bring down a bear," she said.

"Why would I want to poison a bear?"

"You wouldn't want to poison a bear."

"Then why did you say that?"

"Just to make my point."

"I've already forgotten your point."

"You get everything wrong. You can't even cook properly!"

"My cooking is delicious!"

The children's heads snapped back and forth between the witches like they were watching a tennis match. Oliver and Celia were stunned by their father's sudden collapse.

"We're in trouble, Ollie," Celia said.

"Big trouble," Oliver answered.

"We should have made mashed potatoes," the leader said. "Then the children would have eaten it!"

"Kids love yak butter stew!"

"I've had to eat your cooking for over two hundred years. It's enough for me to think about poisoning myself!"

"Why don't you do us all the favor then?!"

"Why don't you make me?!"

"Why don't I!" The leader stood with her fists clenched, staring down the other witch. The others started shouting, trying to break up the fight.

"Is he dead?" Celia whispered while the witches shouted at each other, honking like a gaggle of geese.

"I don't know," said Oliver.

Their father twitched and the witches stopped their argument and turned toward the children in unison, grinning through their pointed teeth. They didn't look like a gaggle of geese anymore. They looked like a group of sharks, which was, appropriately, called a shiver.

"So," the leader said. "We will use the children."

Celia and Oliver gulped and grabbed hands.

Celia tried to step in front of her brother. She was, after all, older by three minutes and forty-two seconds. She had a duty to protect him.

"Use us for what?" Oliver said defiantly. He didn't want the witches to think he was hiding behind his sister.

"You see, young ones, your father is not dead," the leader explained. "Our poison works more slowly, and much more painfully. He is being held in a between-place, between life and death. In five days, when the poison has completed its work, all his good *karma*, all his life force, and all his dreams will pass to us." The witches licked their lips at the thought. "That is how we survive; it is how we have survived for hundreds of years."

"Of course," another witch said, "it does not have to be this way for your father."

"We had wanted to poison you," the woman in the headband said, as if that was supposed to make the twins feel better. "And then your father would have done anything to get the antidote. He would have *found* anything." She smiled widely and nodded to make her point.

"The Lost Tablets," Oliver said.

"You want us to get the Lost Tablets for you,"

Celia said, "and in exchange, you'll give our father the antidote?"

"That's right, child," a witch said. "The tablets will give us control of all the world's knowledge. That's worth quite a lot to trade. No more scrounging in this valley for hikers and pilgrims to poison with yak butter stew. We'll poison priests and kings with cakes and caviar!"

"You must bring us the Lost Tablets before five days are over," the leader said, "or it will be too late."

"How are we supposed to find them?" Oliver asked. "Our father was the explorer. We don't even like going to the park! We don't even like gym class!"

"That is our deal, take or leave it."

"I guess we don't have a choice," Celia said, and Oliver agreed. Their father had wagered their freedom with Sir Edmund and now they had made a deal with the witches.

"The ants go marching two by two," sang the witch who only knew song lyrics. "Hurrah! Hurrah!"

The others laughed and a heavy mist fell around them. A quick wind blew the mist away, and when it cleared, all the witches were gone, along with their huts and the satellite dish, and the logs with the blankets. Even the fire was gone.

"Ummm, Celia," Oliver said.

"Yeah?"

"They took Dad too." He pointed to the empty space where their father's body had been. They stood shivering, not knowing what to do or what to say, or where to go, when the trees rustled. They heard branches cracking.

"What now?" Oliver groaned as he and Celia drew closer together. Whatever came out of the forest, they would face it together. The brush burst open and they squeezed each other's hands tighter, preparing for the worst.

"So," Lama Norbu said as he stepped out of the darkness, his bright smile lighting up the night. He looked around at the empty campsite and furrowed his brow. "What did I miss?"

# 18
# WE NOTICE WHAT
# THE NOTE'S NOT

**THE TWINS EXPLAINED** to Lama Norbu what had happened.

"This is very unfortunate," he said. "I fear we will not have very much success finding the tablets without your father's expertise."

"Our father was poisoned and kidnapped!" Celia yelled. "They're going to steal his soul. I think that's a bit more serious than these silly tablets!"

"These tablets are not silly!" Lama Norbu shouted, and he suddenly didn't sound like Lama Norbu at all. The twins startled, but the monk quickly regained his composure, smiled and spoke softly. "I am sorry for shouting. I, too, am grieving for your father, and this is why we *must* find the

Lost Tablets. They are the only way to save him from the witches . . . that is what I meant."

"Oh," said Celia, still not really convinced Lama Norbu cared at all about her father.

"Well," Oliver said, "would this help?" He ran over to the bushes where the hut with the satellite dish had been and pulled out the little canvas backpack. He reached in and found everything still in it. He took out the page with his mother's writing on it.

"Oh, my, yes!" Lama Norbu exclaimed. "You clever, clever boy!" He hugged Oliver tightly. Oliver stayed stiff as a board. "Good thinking, Oliver. Wonderful!"

Celia just crossed her arms, annoyed that the monk had yelled at her and was now piling praise on her brother's head. She was the one who put the note in the backpack. She was the one who thought to bring the backpack in the first place.

Younger brothers get all the attention, she thought angrily.

"Mom's writing is hard to read," Oliver said, holding up the note. His sister came up next to him to help. "She wrote really weirdly."

" 'NOvember fourth,' " Celia read. " 'liTtle time left; they Are close Behind me, LETting me Search for the Missing pages until they strike. i'm clOser now than i'Ve ImaginEd. No one thought the great lIbrary miGHT be in SHANGRI-LA. only the SHAMANS' EYES can tell the way from here.' "

Oliver thought for a moment. "Why'd she write all weird? And how would the shamans' eyes tell the way? Don't people tell things with their mouths?"

"It's not important right now. Look at the front!" Lama Norbu said impatiently. Oliver glanced at his sister. The monk was acting very un-monk-like, with his shouting and his impatience. Monks on TV didn't act like this at all.

"The Greek writing?" Oliver flipped the paper over and they all looked at the strange symbols and writings.

"Does that mean anything to you?" Lama Norbu asked.

"Nope," Celia said.

"That means 'big books, big evil,' " Oliver said, pointing at the Greek writing. "Dad said so at the Ceremony of Discovery."

"That's the writing that was under that key

symbol in the tunnel at the Explorers Club. It was ancient Greek," said Celia. "Can you read it?"

Lama Norbu scratched his chin and stared at the note, shaking his head.

"Can you read it?" Celia asked again.

"Of course I can!" Lama Norbu snapped at her and snatched the note from Oliver's hands. "Go to sleep now. I must study this privately."

"But our dad only has five days," Celia objected. "We can't just go to sleep. We have to figure this out. He could die!"

"I will do the thinking," Lama Norbu said. "Children need their sleep."

"Where are we supposed to sleep?" Oliver asked. "There's nothing here."

"The hidden lands always provide." Lama Norbu pointed at the bushes and trees around the clearing. "We will build our own shelter."

It was the most exhausting work of their lives, pulling giant waxy leaves from trees and weaving them between sticks and branches. After hours and hours, the twins had built themselves a lean-to and built the monk one too. He spent the whole time looking at their mother's note and muttering to himself.

It turned out that watching hours of *Sell My House!* and *Decorate My House!* and *Build Me a New House!* and *Hey, That's a Really Ugly House!* and all those other house shows that came on Saturday afternoons when cartoons were over had helped them. Celia even put some decorative touches in their lean-to, like colorful flowers on the walls.

"To make the energy better," she explained. She'd heard that on *Decorate My House!* If anyone could use good energy, it was Oliver and Celia. They hadn't slept in ages. They were both happy to put on the change of clothes Celia had made them pack. Even in the creepy jungle of the gorge, it felt good to wear pajamas.

Lama Norbu was sound asleep in minutes and snoring loud enough to wake the entire forest. Neither Oliver nor Celia could sleep, even though they were really tired.

"I'm thinking about Mom's note," Celia said.

"Yeah," replied Oliver. "Can you believe we might be closer to finding her than Dad ever got?"

"Oliver," Celia sighed. "I know you miss her, but she got us into real trouble here." She looked over at her younger-by-three-minutes-and-forty-two-seconds brother, whose glassy eyes gazed back at her in the darkness. "We aren't going to find these tablets."

"But she wrote that note!" Oliver objected. "She left it as a clue and she might still be somewhere, if we can just—"

"Oliver," Celia interrupted. "Mom's note is a trick. That page isn't from any ancient tablets."

"What? How do you know? How can you possibly know that? You don't know that!"

"You know how Mom and Dad used to tell us the stories about the expedition to the North Pole? About how when the two explorers tried to prove they'd been there, they made fake journals so that people would believe they'd done things they hadn't done?"

"Yeah?" Oliver didn't know where his sister was going with this.

"Well, this paper is a fake, just like those journals."

"How do you know that? Why would Mom fake this? Why would she say it's from these Lost Tablets when it isn't?"

"It has something to do with her funny writing," Celia said. "We have to read it again."

"But Lama Norbu has it."

"I don't trust him," Celia said. "He doesn't read Greek."

"So?" Oliver said. "You don't read Greek."

"But I didn't lie about it. He said he could read that page, but it was obvious he couldn't."

"Choden Thordup couldn't read Greek either," Oliver remembered. "Dad always said that real explorers know how to read ancient Greek."

"See?" Celia said. "Something's fishy."

"Hold on," Oliver said. He thought a moment and then, without another word, slipped out of their shelter and snuck over to where the monk was sleeping. The tall monk held the paper on his chest and snored as loud as a yeti's roar. Oliver pulled the paper from the Lama Norbu's hands and scurried back with it to their lean-to. He felt a bit like a superspy.

"Did you see that?" Oliver asked, breathless. "I got it right out from under him. Did you see?"

"Just read it," Celia said.

Oliver started reading the note in the dim light.

NOvember fourth, liTtle time left; they Are close Behind me LETtting me Search for the Missing pages, until they strike. i'm clOser now than i'Ve ImaginEd. No one thought the great lIbrary miGHT be in SHANGRI-LA. only the SHAMANS' EYES can tell the way from here.

"See how the letters are capitalized all weird?" Celia pointed. "It's a code. All the capital letters spell something out."

"How did Dad not notice this?" Oliver wondered.

"The same way you didn't notice when you first looked at the note. He wanted to find her again so badly that he lost his senses a little bit."

"So what's it say?"

Celia used a stick in the dirt to scratch the capital letters in the ground.

"No tablets, movie night, Shangri-La, shamans' eyes," she read.

"No tablets," Oliver gasped. "But if we don't find the tablets, Dad'll die and we'll lose the bet with Sir Edmund and we'll be his slaves."

Celia knew that her brother was right. There was no way to win in this situation.

"What would Agent Zero do?" she asked.

Celia knew just how to get Oliver to feel better. If Agent Zero could deal with assassination attempts, murderous double agents and high school algebra, then Oliver could surely pull himself together and focus too. It was for their father, after all. And for cable television. But really, he thought, looking at his sister, it was for her. It was for what was left of their family.

"Agent Zero would stay calm and figure out how to save Dad," he said. "But how can we do that, if there are no tablets?"

"The rest of the note, maybe?" Celia said. "Movie night, Shangri-La, shamans' eyes?"

"It doesn't mean anything to me," said Oliver. "Maybe she still wants to find Shangri-La and watch a movie there?"

They studied the sketches their mother had drawn. The pictures were a little scary. There were fanged demon things, and there were little arrows going from what looked like yaks to monsters to these two dancing skeletons that were shooting fire out of their eyes. The fire shot from their eyes right into a picture of a waterfall.

"These pictures look like a storyboard," Oliver said.

Celia's eyes brightened. "Like the one Mom gave us. *Escape from the Mummy King*."

"So if this is a storyboard," Oliver asked, "what's it telling us? What's supposed to happen?"

"That's a waterfall, so I think Mom's telling us to go to that waterfall."

"What's with those crazy skeleton things?"

"Maybe they're the shamans we're looking for. Maybe they'll tell us what's going on?"

"Maybe someone should tell *me* what's going on!" Lama Norbu said, pulling open their lean-to and towering over the twins.

"We couldn't sleep!" Celia said quickly. "So we, um—"

"We borrowed the note," Oliver said. "We didn't want to disturb you . . . we thought we could help."

"I see," Lama Norbu said suspiciously. "And did you determine anything?"

"Um, well," Oliver said.

"We should go to the waterfall," Celia answered. "That'll point the way to the tablets."

"Good." Lama Norbu snatched the note back from Celia. "Now go to sleep. We'll leave at first light."

Oliver and Celia looked nervously at each other, but didn't say a word in case the monk was still listening. The only thing they knew for sure at this point was that nothing was as it seemed.

# 19

# WE DESCEND INDECENTLY

**THEY LEFT THEIR MAKESHIFT** camp as the sun came up, after a breakfast of fruit and nuts that Lama Norbu had scrounged from the forest. Oliver smelled the food before eating it to make sure it wasn't poisoned. Celia, who knew from soap operas that good poison couldn't be smelled or tasted, watched Lama Norbu eat first.

Mist still hung heavy over the forest. Birds chirped their morning songs, and monkeys called to each other. The twins stumbled down a narrow path behind Lama Norbu. Celia let Oliver carry the backpack because she was tired. They heard a roar nearby and froze where they stood. Lama Norbu swung his gun from his back and they stood in place for a few minutes, listening to the forest.

"Is that the yeti?" Oliver whispered to his sister.

"Shhhhh," she said.

They waited, but when nothing burst from the mist to attack them, they continued on their way. Some of the bushes and trees had mysterious ribbons tied to them. Others had what looked like hubcaps hanging from their branches.

"Prayer wheels," explained Lama Norbu. "Pilgrims journeying from the valley to the sacred mountains above us will leave these wheels and banners along their path to mark their progress and to bless others who pass this way."

They continued on under the flapping banners and spinning wheels for another hour. The day started to get hotter and stickier. The cold air from the mountains pressed down on the hot air in the valley, coating the forest in a heavy mist that made everything feel like a dream. Shadows moved in the mist and the flapping banners sounded like the whispering of ghosts. This was not a friendly forest. The twins felt like they were being watched.

Suddenly, as they passed through the haze, the path simply ended in front of them. They stood at the edge of a cliff that went straight down to the river at the bottom of the canyon. They could hear the roaring of the Hidden Falls below.

"Where do we go from here?" Celia wondered.

"We must cross the gorge," Lama Norbu said. "I hope you do not fear heights."

He pointed to a thin wire that stretched from one side of the gorge to the other high above the rapids. The other side was at least the length of a football field away.

"I wasn't afraid of heights before," Celia said. "Though I might be now."

Oliver didn't say anything because he could feel his stomach in his throat. The memory of falling out of the airplane was still fresh. Oliver couldn't help but notice that the wire was about as thick as the kind of wire used to hook up cable television. It looked about as sturdy too.

What would Agent Zero do? Oliver thought to himself, and then he remembered that Corey Brandt, the actor in *Agent Zero*, had a stunt double. Agent Zero would probably hang out in his trailer drinking Fanta while someone else took all the risks. Some unlucky kid like Oliver.

Lama Norbu pulled out a few scraps of cloth from his robes and handed them to the twins.

"Wrap these around your palms so the wire doesn't cut into your hands. Then we'll wrap our legs around it, grab on, and scoot across, like you're crawling upside down."

"I don't usually crawl upside down hundreds of feet in the air," said Celia.

Lama Norbu smiled at her and took out his rope. He tied it around each of their waists.

"This way, if one of us falls, the others can catch her," he said.

"What do you mean by *her*?" objected Celia.

Lama Norbu simply shrugged and grabbed on to the wire, swinging his legs up effortlessly and hanging upside down. He began to inch along, trailing the rope behind him. "Come on!" he called back.

"I don't think we should do this," Oliver said.

"He's not trying to trick us," Celia explained. "He went first."

"It's not that. . . . This wire is going to break."

"How do you know that?"

"Every show I've ever watched," he said, "when someone has to cross a gorge or a valley or a canyon . . . the wire or the bridge or whatever always breaks. Always. It's like a law."

"Well, this isn't television," Celia said.

"I know." Oliver sighed. "This is much worse."

The twins wrapped their palms with the cloth and, one after the other, followed Lama Norbu out onto the wire, hanging upside down and crawling along like inchworms. Oliver went first. As always.

The wind whipped past them and made the wire swing and swoop while they crawled. Oliver made the mistake of looking down. The river churned and the air swirled. He felt his hands slipping. His sister shouted to snap him back to attention.

"Hey! This isn't the time for daydreaming! Keep crawling!"

Halfway across, their arms and legs were aching, and they were getting dizzy from hanging upside down for so long. Lama Norbu was whistling a cheery tune while he crawled, but the twins were straining and grunting with the effort. It was like gym class, only with their lives on the line. If this had been a challenge in school, they never would have made it even this far. Lama Norbu called back to encourage them: "The body is only an illusion, and so your pain is not real. Focus and you can accomplish the impossible! In fact, you must."

Just as he said those words, the cloth on his hand tore and he slipped. For a moment, he hung upside down and backwards by his legs, looking Oliver and Celia right in the eyes. It was only for an instant, but his face showed a clear expression both kids knew well from gym class: embarrassment and terror.

A split second later, his legs slipped off the wire and he fell. Oliver watched as if in slow motion as the rope that attached him to Lama Norbu unwound and pulled tight. When the rope had run out, it snapped Oliver right off the wire too and he began to fall behind the monk. Last in the line, Celia watched as her brother fell and the rope connecting them began to pull. She screamed and hugged the wire as tightly as she could, with her arms and legs, vowing that she would not let go no matter how much it hurt.

"Pain is an illusion," she muttered to herself as the full weight of the monk and her brother hung off of her by a gnarly old rope. "An illusion. An illusion. An illusion."

Her grip on the wire was all that stood between the Navel Twins and certain death. She squeezed her eyes shut and held on for dear life against the strain. The wire continued to sway in the wind and her whole body ached and burned against the weight.

"Oliver," Lama Norbu called up, "you must climb back up to the wire. Use the rope and climb!"

"Hang on, Sis!" Oliver yelled as he reached one hand over the other and started to climb. Now it really was like gym class.

"Ahhhh!" Celia yelled as the shifting weight yanked her waist. She tried to clear her mind, to think about anything else. She started to list the television networks they'd have once they got cable: "ABC, BET, CBS, FOX, HBO, NBC, TBS, TNT, USA, Cartoon Network, Soap Network, Reality Network, Reality Two, Reality Three, Food Network, All Sports, All Sports Except Fishing, The Fishing Network . . . Ahhhh!"

Oliver was halfway up to his sister when his arms slipped and he went skidding down the rope, burning his palms. He couldn't give up, though. He began again, one hand over the other.

His arms ached from lifting himself and Lama Norbu below him. Every muscle in his body strained and screamed at him, but he had to speed up. He didn't know how much longer his sister

could hang on to the full weight of two people. Overhead, giant vultures had gathered, swirling through the warm air, hoping to catch a meal.

Celia thought of every television show she had ever seen; she imagined what was on right now; she tried to list her favorite actors in alphabetical order; tried to imagine Cory Brandt cheering her on. Anything to distract her from the pain. It wasn't working.

Then she thought of her mother.

Her mother had climbed Mount Everest when she was only eighteen years old. Her mother had trekked alone through the jungles of South America, had swum with great white sharks in South Africa, had told Celia bedtime stories and rubbed her stomach when she was sick, sang ancient songs of healing from the Twa People of Rwanda to her, and blessed her with secret prayers from Kabbalah.

Celia was her mother's daughter. Her mother had always believed in her. And if her mother could believe in her, then she would not fall!

As she imagined her mother's face, watching her, she forgot all about the pain and the danger and the fear. All she knew was that she was loved, and for the first time, she was sure, absolutely sure, that her mother was alive somewhere. She couldn't explain how she knew, she just did. Before she realized any time had passed, there was Oliver, red-faced and soaked in sweat, hanging from the wire next to her.

"Hey, Sis," Oliver panted. "Coach Busick would never have believed we could do that, huh?" He even managed a smile. Lama Norbu hung from the wire right behind him. Celia noticed that the weight on her arms wasn't so intense anymore. They felt like Jell-O, sure, but they were also relieved; her brother had taken the weight off of her. Celia let out a breath and simply laughed. Even though she was still hanging like laundry hundreds of feet in the air over wild river rapids, she had never felt so relieved in her life.

The moment didn't last.

With a terrible splitting sound and deep vibrating *twaaaang*, the strands of the wire, which had hung across the gorge for almost a hundred years, started to break.

*Twang! Twang! Twang!*

The wire jerked and jolted with every snapping strand.

"Hurry," yelled Lama Norbu, as they all tried to scurry as fast as they could toward the other side of the gorge.

"Go faster!" Oliver yelled, but it was too late. With one terrible snap, the old wire broke off from the cliff, and they swung down through the air like monkeys on a vine, except they were going way too fast and heading right for a wall of solid rock. Jagged boulders jutted out at them, like the spikes in the Cabinet of Count Vladomir next to their fridge at home. If they held on, they would be impaled.

Celia looked down at the raging river below and saw their only choice. As desperately as she had held on moments before, she let go. Oliver was yanked right off the wire after her, followed by Lama Norbu.

"Ahhhh!" they all screamed as they fell backward toward the frothing river below, tied to each other and flapping their arms like flightless birds,

# 20

# WE DON'T QUESTION THE WISDOM OF RAINBOWS

**THE OLD ABBOT OF THE** Monastery of the Demon Fortress of the Oracle King knelt beside the calm pool at the base of the Hidden Falls. He had traveled for weeks, eating only a grain of rice a day. He was tired, but his spirit felt fresh and young. He had reached the goal of his pilgrimage, the place that had appeared to him in a dream. He removed a small butter lamp from his bag and set it on the ground.

"For as long as space endures, and for as long as living beings remain, until then may I too stay to heal the misery of the world," he chanted. It was his favorite saying from the sacred texts. He bowed his head to the earth and rose again to light the lamp.

The flame flickered in the cool air. Behind him,

the Hidden Falls rose hundreds of feet, and, in the mist where the water crashed into a pool at its base, a rainbow blossomed. The abbot smiled.

For months, the monks at his monastery had been afflicted by horrible nightmares. Though his monastery had a terrible-sounding name, it was a place of peace, reflection and learning. There were no demons there, and it looked more like a medieval spa than a fortress. No one actually knew how it had come to have that name, but for centuries the monks had prayed and studied there, hidden from the modern world. Outsiders imagined the place was Shangri-La, as if such a place existed. To the abbot it was simply home.

But all that changed a few months ago. One of their monks, a powerful oracle who channeled the spirit of their protector, Dorjee Drakden, had vanished. Then the nightmares spread like wildfire.

Now, hundreds of sleepless monks were wandering the halls. Everyone was so tired and nervous from the dreams that small arguments turned into ugly fights very quickly. If a monk coughed too loudly or ommed too quietly, all of their nonviolence training went right out the window. Fists would fly. The abbot had never thought he would have to break up fights or treat bloody noses. He felt like a nurse and a referee more than a wise and learned abbot. It was a terrible situation.

The monks' nightmares were all the same, and the abbot suffered from them too. In the dream, Dorjee Drakden, their great protector, was locked in a cage, helpless, as an army of men marched across the land, setting fire to all in their path. The leader of that army carried a giant scroll wrapped in chains, and scholars threw their sacred texts in front of him. He stomped them into the dirt.

"Has the protector abandoned us?" frightened monks would ask the abbot in the morning. "Will we be destroyed?"

The abbot could not say, but he decided to take a pilgrimage to find out. As he walked for days and days, down from his mountain and into the hidden lands, he meditated, hoping that he would find guidance. He saw an image of these great waterfalls, of the pool beneath, and of three rainbows. He decided he would go to the place in his visions. He had arrived and now he would meditate.

"Ommmmm," he said.

He pictured the ferocious protector-spirits of Tibet, in all their many forms. He pictured Dorjee Drakden. He pictured the Chitipati, the dancing skeleton twins who guard the burial grounds of eternity and protect the righteous from thieves. The Chitipati feared nothing, not even the other spirits. If the abbot could meditate on them to defeat fear, then so could all his monks, and so could all people. It was a big task he'd set for himself. He would need to concentrate. This was some of the hardest meditation a person could do. It was dangerous to invoke the ferocious protectors if you were not ready. He lit another butter lamp.

"Ommmm," he said. *"Ommmmm."*

"Ahhhhhhh," he heard in response. *"Ahhhhhhhhhh!"*

His heart quickened. Could this be the response he had hoped for? Could this be the answer of the gods? What did it mean?

*"Ommmmmm,"* he said again.

*"Ahhhhhhhhhh!"* he heard again. And again. *"Ahhhhhhhhhh!"*

The voice was not from his head. It came from behind him. He sighed. His concentration was broken. All this strange shouting was quite distracting. He turned toward the falls to see what all the trouble was about.

Just then, he saw a small form fly over the edge. It looked like a monk shouting and waving his arms frantically. Behind the monk another small form fell, shouting. This one looked like a child with a school backpack. And it was tied to the monk. And then a third form, tied to the other two, also plunged over the edge of the falls. That one looked like a little girl. All three shouted as they fell.

"AHHHHHHHHHHHHH!"

He watched the three figures, flailing and falling through the water and the mist, as they crashed into the deep pool. He waited to see what would happen next. Just as three heads popped out of the water, choking and gagging, he saw that the rainbow above them had split into three, just like he had seen in his vision.

This is what he was meant to see. These three figures would end the nightmares that had plagued his monks and would restore the protector to his place. The abbot packed up his lamps and rose. He had a long trek back to his monastery on the icy mountain. He could hardly wait to tell his followers the good news.

He couldn't actually imagine how a monk and two children had come to crash over the Hidden Falls, nor how they would be of any help, but he had long ago learned not to question the wisdom of dreams or rainbows, and certainly not to interfere with their plans.

He took one last look across the water, being careful not to be seen, and watched as the children climbed out of the water and yanked the sopping wet monk out behind them. They slumped down on the bank, exhausted, and the abbot was again tempted to run over and bless them, to ask them who they were and why they were there. He wanted to help them. But he resisted. All would be clear in time, he told himself, and they had their own journey to complete. He turned and started his trek out of the valley, walking as fast as he could. The three rainbows faded behind him.

# 21
# WE KNOW HE'S NO LAMA

**OLIVER AND CELIA SCRAMBLED** out of the water at the bottom of the great waterfall. Their clothes were dirty, dripping and torn, and every inch of them was soaked. Oliver took off the wet backpack and set it on the rocks with a plop. They watched as three rainbows faded into the foam.

"We're alive!" Oliver shouted and jumped up and down.

"What?" Celia shouted. The roar of the waterfall made talking almost impossible.

Oliver just smiled and hugged his sister. A line of butterflies fluttered overhead, dancing and swirling in the air.

The twins had seen waterfalls on television before, but this was something else entirely.

"Wow," Oliver said.

"Wow," Celia said.

The water crashed down hundreds of feet into the pool in front of them. The mist and water and shimmering remains of the rainbows were beautiful. Celia couldn't help feeling bad that their father wasn't around to see it. He would have loved a sight like this. And she couldn't help but wonder if her mother had really been here. This was the kind of place that explorers loved to discover. Neither one of them could think of a TV show to compare this to. They were dumbstruck.

Lama Norbu sat on the bank of the river, exhausted, with his feet dangling in the water. The twins were so busy admiring the butterfly parade and trying to think of something they'd seen on TV that was as amazing as this waterfall that they didn't see him fiddling with the wet phone in his lap, banging on it and cursing under his breath. He eventually gave up trying to get it to work and tossed it into the river. Frank Pfeffer did not care about littering. He sighed and stood.

"We've arrived," he declared, and pointed at the waterfall, as if the twins might not have noticed. "The ruined monastery is just behind this screen of water. We'll have to climb up the rocks over there to get to it."

The twins were tired of climbing, because it always ended up with a lot of falling, but they were so close to their goal, they didn't complain. They just turned and started on their way up, scrambling and sliding over wet boulders.

They slipped behind the thunderous wall of falling water and found themselves in a large cavern. Sunlight passing through the waterfall made it look like glowing marble, rather than tons and tons of crashing water.

"Why would someone want to build a monastery down here?" Celia asked.

"It's kind of a cool place," Oliver said. "I bet *Secrets of the Underworld* would love to do an episode here."

"I never want to watch that show again," Celia said. "I've had enough reality for a while."

"Reality TV is different," Oliver objected. "It's not as wet as real reality."

Celia just shrugged. She couldn't understand boys sometimes.

The cave itself wasn't just rock and moss, like a normal cave. It had once been built into something. There were doorways that led into other passages. Some of the doorways were filled with broken doors hanging off their frames, others just had piles of rock and ash where wooden doors used to be. The walls were charred too, like someone had tried to burn down the inside of the mountain, and soot covered up elaborate murals painted on the walls.

Oliver and Celia were able to make out strange images of men sitting on clouds, and tigers leaping over hills and rivers, but the images were all broken and burned. There was a stairwell at the back of the cave that descended into the shadows and there was a statue in front of the stairs that looked like someone had tried to break it.

"This place is creepy," Celia said, and Oliver did not disagree. He shivered.

The statue in front of them was of twin skeletons. Their mouths were open and filled with long, razor-sharp fangs. They were dancing and holding strange objects in their claws. They each had an extra eye in the middle of their foreheads and they each wore a crown of tiny skulls. Everywhere Celia stepped in the cave, she felt as if the skeletons were watching her through their third eyes. The eyes seemed to glow.

"The Chitipati," Lama Norbu explained. "Guardians of the charnel grounds."

"What's a charnel ground?" Oliver asked.

"The place where the bodies of the dead are burned."

Both twins looked back at the statues and shuddered.

"Not cool," Oliver said.

"This was the monastery of the Ferocious Protectors," Lama Norbu said. "Here they prayed to the warrior-god Dorjee Drakden. These skeleton twins are meant to protect the righteous against thieves. If ever there were a place to hide the Lost Tablets of Alexandria, this would be it. We must try to decipher what your mother told us," Lama Norbu said.

He pulled the page out from his robes. It was soaking wet and the ink had blurred. A few runny demon faces from the sketch were still visible, an arm or two, but little else.

"No!" the monk suddenly shouted, his face changed into a mask of rage. The children jumped. His voice echoed through the chamber, as if there were an army of monks shouting "No!" over and over. Lama Norbu didn't even look like a monk anymore. He looked younger and even taller, and angry. "WHAT AM I SUPPOSED TO DO WITH THIS? I HAVE NOT COME THIS FAR TO FAIL!"

"It's okay," Oliver said consolingly. "It wasn't really a Lost Tablet. There are no—"

"Shhh," Celia hushed her brother. Lama Norbu snapped his head toward the twins.

"You have no idea what you're talking about," he shouted, and approached them angrily. "This page is real! It must be! I stole it from your mother myself!"

"What?"

"You stole—"

"We followed your mother here all the way from the Gobi Desert!" Lama Norbu shouted.

"What?" said Oliver.

"We?" said Celia.

"Me and Janice!" snapped Lama Norbu, who now didn't look at all like a monk.

"You mean you're Frank Pfeffer, from the Pfeffer/McDermott Expedition?!" Celia cried. She felt like a fool. She had known something strange was going on with this monk from the beginning.

"You're not a lama at all!" Oliver shouted. He remembered the way Celia had pressed his face into the word *toothpicks* on that statue in the library.

"Oh, will you shut up with this llama business! I explained that already."

"I mean that you aren't a monk at all!"

"You've found me out," Lama Norbu/Frank Pfeffer admitted with a dark smile. "Oh, it feels good not to pretend anymore. I really hate acting." He stood up taller and peeled the thin white mustache off his face. His voice changed and he seemed to transform from an old monk to a much bigger man. An explorer. "Janice and I found your mother after her dirigible crashed. We wanted to help her, but she was too stubborn."

"Dirigible?" Oliver mouthed at his sister.

"Blimp," she responded.

"We told your mother that we would bring her home to her family in exchange for what she'd found, but she refused. She said that she was not about to turn over her discovery to 'common grave robbers.' She actually called us that. And some other not very nice things."

Oliver and Celia were now very worried. They

had heard about grave robbers for years. They'd seen shows about them, of course. They were criminals who found ancient tombs and cemeteries and dug up bodies and stole whatever valuable things they found. On TV, it was kind of exciting and kind of creepy. But in real life, grave robbers were not exciting and were much worse than creepy. Their father had been clubbed on the head by grave robbers in Peru just a few months ago. It made his ears ring for a month. Oliver did not want to get clubbed on the head or have his ears ring. He needed his ears for hearing the TV. He liked his ears, even if Celia pulled him around by them sometimes.

"We were very insulted," Lama Norbu/Frank Pfeffer said. "We are certainly not grave robbers."

Oliver was relieved. His ears already felt safer.

"We only robbed *from* grave robbers. We let them do the hard work. . . . All that digging is not for me. Who wants to go hunting in caves for toothpicks? Ugh."

Oliver was not relieved anymore. Someone who robbed *from* grave robbers was even worse than grave robbers.

"You're not even an explorer," Celia said. "You're just a thief."

"Don't sound so shocked. What do you think your parents do? They are famous for robbing graves. Just because they give what they find to museums doesn't make them any less grave robbers."

"Our parents are *explorers*," Oliver said. Celia couldn't believe her brother was defending explorers. It was explorers who had gotten them into this mess.

"Whatever she was, we followed your mother all the way to this cave," Frank Pfeffer said. "If she wasn't going to give us her discovery, we were going to take it from her. I waited for her to come out. I waited for days, but she didn't. Weeks passed. It was so boring, sitting for so long in this gorge, watching monks come and go. So I decided to flush her out. I started a little fire."

"You started the fire?" Celia asked. "With our mother inside!"

"Oh, with lots of people inside. There were over a hundred monks living here. They all left when the fire went out of control. All but your mother.

She never came out. I went to look in the ashes when morning came, but I didn't find her. I didn't even find her body. But I found this page. I couldn't read it. What do I know about ancient Greek? But I knew someone who did."

"Dad!" Celia said.

"That's right. We knew your father would see this note your mother wrote and work tirelessly to track her down. And if we followed, we'd be led right to the tablets! So Janice went to the Ceremony of Discovery disguised as Choden Thordup."

"I knew something was wrong with her!" Celia shouted. "Neither of you are really from Tibet! There's no such person as Lama Norbu or Choden Thordup."

"What about the yak?" Oliver asked. "The one she named Stephen?"

"For someone who watches so much television," Frank Pfeffer sneered, "you aren't very good at recognizing make-believe." He laughed. "We just told your father what he needed to hear. We made a deal with Sir Edmund to sell him the tablets when we found them. *You two* were supposed to be poisoned so your father would work for us. But instead, those witches poisoned *him*, and now I'm stuck with you: *Oliver and Celia the couch potatoes!*"

"We aren't couch potatoes!" Oliver shouted.

"We are *audiovisual enthusiasts*," Celia said. She'd seen those words in an advertisement for flat-screen TVs. She didn't know exactly what they meant, but it sure sounded better than couch potatoes. "And you're a *charlatan*," she added, because if there was ever a time to call someone a faker, a liar and a fraud, it was right at this moment.

# 22

# WE'RE SHOWN SOME SHAMANS

"**WELL, WHATEVER I AM,**" Frank Pfeffer snapped at Celia, "it is now up to you to help me. I will not return empty-handed."

"Why would we help you?" Oliver demanded. "You lied to us and you tried to set fire to our mother. You're working with Sir Edmund."

"You will help me because I am the only one who knows how to save your father from the Poison Witches and you're running out of time. If the witches don't kill him, Sir Edmund certainly will. I am your only hope."

Oliver's shoulders slumped. For two people who didn't like to leave the couch, he and Celia sure had a lot of enemies all of a sudden.

"Well, *you're* the explorer," Celia said. "How are we supposed to help you?"

"I have no earthly idea, but I believe that with the right motivation, young people can accomplish anything. And I would think your father's life is motivation enough. So start looking."

"What are we even looking for if there are no tablets?" Oliver wondered.

"The way to Shangri-La, then," Frank Pfeffer said. "Find that for me."

"We'll need the paper," answered Oliver. "It's the only clue we have."

"I can't imagine what you'll see." Frank shrugged as he handed them the wet document. Oliver threw the backpack onto his back and held the paper in front of him as they started to wander. The runny sketches looked just like the burnt images on the walls of the cave.

"Mom drew this right here," Oliver said, comparing a runny image on the paper with a burnt image on the ceiling.

Frank Pfeffer leaned against the wall and picked at his teeth with a little jade toothpick he pulled out of his pocket.

"So what do we do?" Oliver whispered.

"I might have an idea," Celia said.

"Hey!" Frank Pfeffer shouted. "Less chatting and more searching."

They wandered up and down the length of the chamber, peering through the dark doorways. Every room held a different strange and ferocious statue. Fanged monks sitting cross-legged on giant flowers; horned demons with many arms and many legs devouring human bodies; strange beasts surrounded by puddles of melted wax from what were once candles. The place creeped Celia out. It made Oliver think of all the scary movies he'd ever seen.

"Don't go anywhere," he warned Celia.

"What?"

"When girls run off alone in horror movies, bad things happen."

"Just keep looking, Oliver. I can take care of myself," she answered, but she did stay closer to her brother. It was better to be safe than sorry, she thought.

As they peered into another dark room, Oliver leaned on the charred door frame. It cracked with a loud noise and he tumbled over into the room.

That's when the ceiling started screeching.

"Uh-oh," he said.

Thousands of bats swooped down and swirled around them. Celia swatted and swung to keep them out of her hair as they darted to and fro. She dove down to the floor next to her brother. By the thousands the bats rushed toward the roaring water at the front of the cave. In the distance, they heard Frank Pfeffer scream.

"Now is our chance to get away!" Celia said. "Run to the stairs at the back of the cave."

Both children bolted upright and ran in the opposite direction from the bats, ducking low and swatting in front of them to keep the way clear. They kept getting hit in the face by low-flying bats.

"Ahhh!" Oliver yelled. "I hate bats!"

"I thought you hated lizards!" Celia shouted back.

"Can't I hate both?"

They made their way to the back stairs and just as they were about to rush down into the darkness to escape, Celia stopped and grabbed her brother by the ear, yanking him backwards.

"Ouch," he yelled. "Why'd you do that?"

"It's a projector!" Celia shouted.

"What?"

Celia pointed at the statue of the skeleton twins

that stood between them and the entrance to the cave. They were looking at its back. From behind they could see what looked like a switch on the back of each statue. They could see that the third eyes didn't just *seem* to glow . . . they did glow. There were little crystals in the backs of the skeleton's heads that shined with light.

"Movie night!" Celia said.

"What are you two doing?" Frank Pfeffer yelled. He was swatting and ducking to avoid the bats, trying to get closer to the twins.

Oliver and Celia didn't answer. They stepped to the back of the statue and looked at the switches and at each other.

"Mom always said that movie projectors were like shamans, showing us stories and distant worlds."

"Maybe that's what she meant in the note," Celia said. "She wrote that note so that only we could understand it! She wanted *us* to find this projector. That's *our* shaman! Movie night *and* shamans' eyes! Maybe that will show us the way to Shangri-La!"

Celia flipped the switch on the back of one of the statues and light shot from its third eye into the back of the white waterfall. The waterfall was just like a giant screen. The statue was like an old film projector. The whole place looked like it was set up just for them, their own movie theater at the bottom of the world.

"Mom," Oliver whispered, amazed, and Celia just nodded.

"What if . . . ," Oliver said, and reached up with the wet piece of paper and slid it into a slot carved out of one of the statue heads. At first they saw a giant image of a runny ink blob projected on the back of the waterfall. Oliver flipped the switch on the back of the other statue and its third eye also lit up. Suddenly, a picture snapped into focus on the back of the falls. It was a picture of the Navel family sitting on their couch together, years before their mom had gone. Both kids gasped and Frank Pfeffer stared at the image, awestruck. The last of the bats flew right out through the picture.

"How . . ." was all Frank Pfeffer said.

Oliver pulled the paper out of the slot and looked at it. It looked like a wet piece of parchment, but when he put it back in the slot and the light from the skeleton's crystal eye passed through it, the image appeared again.

"This was the clue Mom left," Celia said. "She left it for you and me, not for Dad."

"But look, that picture's not right," Oliver said. In the image they were all sitting on the couch smiling, but hanging on the wall where their storyboard from *Escape from the Mummy King* was framed, there was a painting instead. It was a painting of a monastery on a mountain. It looked almost like the flags were flapping in the breeze. Their mother also had on a piece of jewelry the kids had never seen her wearing before, a necklace with an image of a key on it. The same weird symbol they'd seen over and over again.

"The Monastery of the Demon Fortress of the Oracle King," Frank Pfeffer gasped. He was looking at the picture on the wall and not paying any attention to their mother's necklace. "Of course! The greatest scribes in all of Tibet live there in total isolation. That would be the perfect place for the tablets to be hidden! That could be Shangri-La itself! Thank you, children."

Frank Pfeffer smiled cruelly and came toward the kids, who stepped back, slipping a little on the floor of the cave. It was hard to walk backward and they kept stumbling and catching each other.

The floor was uneven and wet and covered in bat poop. If you have never walked backward through wet bat poop, you should know that it's not easy. I don't recommend it without special shoes. Oliver and Celia did not have special shoes. Just sneakers. They nearly fell over altogether.

Frank Pfeffer reached up to the skeleton statue and snatched the paper from its slot and shoved it into his pocket. He looked down on the twins.

"What happens now?" Celia demanded.

"You watch enough television," he said. "You must be experts at figuring out what happens next. Why don't you tell me?"

"You're going to leave us here," Oliver said.

"Exactly."

"And then you're going to the Demon Fortress of Whatever for yourself," Celia continued. "And you'll let the Poison Witches take our father."

"You are exactly right." Frank Pfeffer laughed. "Television has not rotted your brains completely, it seems."

"Except you forgot something," Celia said. "Just when things seem really bad at the end of an episode, there is always a twist. And we have a twist for you."

"We do?" Oliver wondered.

"We do," Celia said, and charged like a football player at Frank Pfeffer's waist.

"Ahhhh," he shouted as her shoulders slammed into him and he stepped back to brace himself. His foot landed right in a pile of bat poop, which you now know is very slippery. Frank Pfeffer was not wearing special bat-poop hiking shoes either, and he fell over backward and slid. Celia shot up from on top of him and ran toward her brother.

"Ahhhh," Frank Pfeffer screamed as he crashed into the waterfall at the cave's entrance.

"Go to the stairs!" she yelled, and Oliver reached back, grabbed her hand and pulled her toward the dark stairs at the back of the cave.

"That . . . was . . . your . . . big plan?" Oliver huffed, taking two steps down at time and using the wall as a guide in the pitch black. "To push him?"

"To push him into bat poop," Celia corrected. "I didn't say it was a good plan. But I didn't hear any ideas from you, Agent Zero."

"I was thinking. That's what secret agents do. They don't just push people."

"We escaped, didn't we?"

"You call this escaping?" Oliver said as he stopped and his sister bumped into him from behind. They didn't know how far they had gone down or how far they had left to go. They were surrounded by darkness.

"I don't think he's coming after us," Celia said. "I think we made it—"

"Shhhh!" Oliver cut her off. "Whenever someone says that, something terrible happens!"

"Stop being stupid."

"You didn't believe me about the wire, and look what happened!"

"Yeah, but this is different. I mean, he's not chasing us. So that's good."

Just as Celia said that, a flashlight popped on next to them, revealing Frank Pfeffer standing right above, inches away, soaking wet and bruised and slimy with bat poop. Shadows danced ghoulishly across his cruel smile. A painting of a three-eyed demon glowed on the wall next to him.

"Oh, no," Celia said.

"Told ya," said Oliver.

"Of course, bat poop and waterfalls won't stop me." He laughed. "And now . . . a push for a push."

And with that, he raised his hand and froze just

before hitting Celia. He smirked, extended his index finger, and pushed on the third eye in the painting on the wall next to him. It sunk into the wall with a creak. The stairs shook a little and bits of dust and rock fell. There was a moment of silence and Frank Pfeffer wrinkled his brow. Suddenly, with a loud crack, the stairs below Oliver and Celia crumbled. Frank laughed as they plummeted into the darkness.

## 23

# WE ARE TRAPPED

**FALLING INTO THE DARK** is very different from falling out of an airplane or falling into a gorge or falling over a waterfall. If people reviewed falling the way they reviewed movies, they might say that falling out of an airplane was "equal parts thrilling and terrifying, four stars!" and that falling into a gorge was "dangerous and unpleasant, three and a half stars" and that falling over a waterfall was "the wettest thing you'll ever do, two stars. Not recommended for children or people with heart conditions."

Falling into the dark surrounded by crumbled stone stairs, however, is completely different, as the twins quickly discovered. Two thumbs down. No stars. It's just bad.

As soon as the stairs broke apart, the twins felt themselves lurch into the air and fall away from the glow of Frank Pfeffer's flashlight and his devilish smile. They didn't know if they were falling a hundred feet down onto a bed of spikes, or sixteen feet onto a feather mattress. They couldn't see the floor.

This is it, Oliver thought. We're dead. I'll never see the TV again, or my sister or my parents. I'll never get a television in my room or go to college or know how *Agent Zero* ends.

I failed, Celia thought as she fell. I couldn't save my brother or my father, or find my mother, or get us cable. And now we're going to die in some Tibetan pit because an evil grave robber pretending to be a monk broke the stairs.

"I'm sorry, Oliver!" she called out in the darkness. "I'm sorry that I . . . oooof!"

She landed with a hard thud, and right next to her she heard what sounded like a sack of flour hitting the ground and knew her brother had landed with an *oooooof* right on the backpack. Stones and dust rained down on them and Celia covered her face with her arms. They hadn't fallen that far at all and the ground was dirt below them, softer than stone. They'd be bruised, but they were alive. Gravity just couldn't kill the Navel Twins.

Celia was so relieved she started laughing. She was lying on her back looking up at the glow from Frank Pfeffer's flashlight.

"Are you okay?" Oliver groaned. The wind had been knocked out of him. He brushed bits of crumbled stairs off himself.

Celia didn't answer; she just kept laughing. Oliver couldn't help but find his sister totally incomprehensible sometimes.

"Enjoy your time together," Frank Pfeffer yelled down at them. "You will quickly find that there is no way out of this pit. I expect you'll starve within a few days. Too bad about saving your father. Oh, well. I highly recommend you use the time you have left to meditate. Perhaps you'll be reborn as a llama! With two ls of course!"

He cackled hysterically and then tossed the flashlight down to them as he left. It landed with a clatter and lit up the ground around them.

The light flickered and cast an eerie glow into the alcoves that ringed the round chamber. The pit had been some kind of meditation room. There were eight alcoves and each contained the sooty ruins of broken statues. Most were burned beyond recognition, but one remained almost unharmed.

It held a statue of a ferocious demon with giant fangs and six arms holding snakes and spears riding a roaring lion. The creature had a third eye in the center of his forehead, just like the skeleton twins. He looked like he was charging into battle.

"You think this is one of those ferocious protector gods?" Oliver asked nervously.

"I guess so," Celia said. "Though his protection didn't do us much good."

"Maybe it's like the lama said," Oliver suggested. "We have to meditate and ask for his help."

"Are you nuts? The lama wasn't even a lama! That was Frank Pfeffer! He was probably lying about everything."

"I know, but just because something's made-up doesn't mean we can't learn from it," Oliver said. "Think about *Love at 30,000 Feet*. It saved us with the witches."

"Are you serious? You don't even know how to meditate." Oliver was right, but she wasn't ready to lose this argument.

"How hard can it be?"

Celia just crossed her arms and tapped her foot, annoyed. She couldn't think of a better idea. There really was no way out of this dark pit, and if the demon statue could help them, why not try it. She hated to give in to her brother, but she figured it was her fault they got pushed into the pit, so she owed him one.

"Okay," she agreed. "What do we do?"

"Well, we sit cross-legged facing the statue. Whenever anyone does this on TV, they always sit up really straight and rest their hands on their knees and close their eyes. Like this." He demonstrated. When he opened one eye to see if his sister was doing it, she was still standing with her arms folded. "Come on, you have to do it right."

Celia sighed and assumed the position next to her brother. The statue towered over them. Oliver shifted uncomfortably on his butt. He thought about his father lying unconscious as a prisoner of the Poison Witches. He thought about how his mother had been here, maybe in this very room. How she had left a projector, as if she knew they would look for her. He thought about becoming Sir Edmund's slave. He thought about Frank Pfeffer and how he had seemed like such a nice monk. His knees hurt from the weird position he was sitting in and he guessed that thinking about all the bad stuff going on wasn't how this was supposed to work. He tried to clear his head, but he couldn't stop thinking about *Ducks Incorporated*, a cartoon he used to love about a family of ducks who ran a giant computer company.

He peeked over at his sister. Her brow was wrinkled in concentration and her lips were moving like she was praying. Oliver couldn't believe how much she looked like the martial arts experts on the training episode of *Agent Zero*. How come she had a talent for meditation and he didn't?

As he watched her lips move, he noticed the words she was muttering. They weren't like any prayer he could imagine.

"High up in the sky . . . love's a look in your eye . . . so climb on board . . . play a chord . . . and fall in lo-ove. Lo-ove . . . lo-ove."

"Hey," Oliver interrupted his sister. "You aren't meditating! That's the theme song to *Love at 30,000 Feet!*"

"It's all I can think of. Meditation is hard."

"Yeah," Oliver agreed.

"You'd think we'd be good at sitting still and staring."

"Like when you made me watch the *Love at*

*30,000 Feet* marathon. We must have sat still for like fifty hours."

"Fifty-two, and yeah, that was great."

"That was horrible. I can't believe I had to endure that."

"Oh, come on! It's a great show and you know it. You even said that Captain Sinclair was kind of cool. And you just said it's what saved us from the Poison Witches."

"That's it!" Oliver shouted.

"What? Captain Sinclair? The witches? What?"

"No! Not Captain Sinclair! Not the witches! The yak! The yak's message! Again!"

"Why are you always shouting about yaks?"

"That yak might just be the smartest talking animal I've ever dreamed about."

"You dream about a lot of talking animals?"

Oliver ignored his sister. She was always coming up with the ideas and trying to protect him, but this time, he figured it out. He knew just what to do. He felt like a Zen master. Agent Zero would have been proud.

"Listen, I know just what to do," he said.

## 24

# WE'RE BEING WATCHED

**ON A HIGH BOULDER** at the top of the waterfall stood Sir Edmund with a group of six women
whose teeth were filed down to razor-sharp points
and whose skin was withered and craggy like a
map of the gorge itself. They called themselves
the *Dugmas*, but the twins called them the Poison
Witches.

Together, they watched the water crashing
below them and saw a tall man slip out from the
cave behind the wall of white water. He was alone,
with a gun slung on his back. His clothes were
wet and covered with what looked bat poop.

"Norbu," the lead witch with the jeweled turquoise headband said.

"You can stop calling him that, I think," Sir
Edmund answered her. "No one is around who can
hear us." They all looked back at the form lying

on the ground behind them. Dr. Navel was still and silent, his breath moving very slowly in and out as if he was just barely clinging to life. "Frank Pfeffer has done well. He seems to know where he's going now."

"What of the children?" the lead witch asked.

Sir Edmund just shrugged.

"If they still live, they will do all they can to find the tablets before Norb—I mean, Pfeffer. That does not worry you?" she asked.

"I should have told you ladies earlier," Sir Edmund said, "but there are no Lost Tablets. They were destroyed long ago. I saw to it personally."

"What?" the witch exclaimed. The others gasped. They clapped in Sir Edmund's face, which in Tibet was not a nice thing to do. These were some unhappy witches. "How dare you lie to us?"

"Don't be so surprised. *You* lie to everyone you meet. I won't have a lesson on the Golden Rule from witches who poison people around their campfire."

"But we made a deal with you."

"Our deal still stands. You get this explorer's soul," Sir Edmund said, and pointed at Dr. Navel. "In fact, you are guaranteed to get it, as the children cannot bring you something that does not exist, can they?"

"But . . ." The leader scratched her head, puzzled. While she was an excellent murderer and stealer of souls, she had never been to school or played chess or watched an episode of *Agent Zero*. She couldn't think about complicated plans. She pretty much knew how to mix poisons into a small number of yak butter stew recipes. Plotting was not her strong suit.

"When Frank and his partner came to me with that piece of paper, I saw immediately that the note hid a code from the mother of those bratty kids, but I didn't know what the rest the code really meant. I *did* know that Frank and his partner wanted revenge on the Navel family, and that Dr. Navel could not resist a chance to find his wife. I simply had to push him into it with my little bet, to get him to bring his kids and let them figure out what that code meant."

"So you don't even know what you are searching for?" the witches asked, shocked.

"Oh, it isn't obvious? I am searching for the children's mother. I believe she copied the tablets before I was able to destroy them. I must have that copy. That catalog is the most important clue to finding the Lost Library. The Council must be the only ones who possess it."

One of the witches hissed and the rest clapped again. They didn't like Sir Edmund very much. Not many people did.

"I had thought it would be easier to find this woman, of course. I hadn't expected the Navels to be thrown off the plane or that Pfeffer might try to change our deal, but all is well again. I will find her and I will get what I want."

"And what about what we want?"

"Apologies," Sir Edmund said, though it was obvious he wasn't really apologizing. "Come with me after Frank Pfeffer, and when I have what I want, you can have Frank's soul too. How does that sound? Two explorers for the price of one."

"And the children?"

"No." Sir Edmund smirked. "I will keep the children. I have something *else* in mind for them. Their work is far from over."

The leader held up her finger to Sir Edmund, demanding silence. She turned and huddled with the other witches and they murmured to each other like a football team planning a play. They talked for a very long time, while Sir Edmund kept checking his watch, which had a symbol of a scroll in chains on it, and looking down at the tiny form of Frank Pfeffer climbing the walls of the canyon. At last, the witches turned around again.

"We have consulted," the leader said gravely.

"And . . . ," Sir Edmund prompted. She puffed up her chest and looked as though she was about to make an important pronouncement.

"Sure," she said at last.

Sir Edmund shook his head. "All right, so we follow wherever he goes and you do as I say until we get there."

"Agreed," the leader said. "But . . . there is a problem."

"Oh, what now!?" Sir Edmund threw his tiny arms in the air in exasperation.

"We are forbidden to leave this valley. Ever since the protector-spirit banished the unruly gods in ancient times, we have been confined to this valley."

"Ha!" Sir Edmund scoffed. "*That's* your worry? Dorjee Drakden is my prisoner now. I have locked up his oracle. We talked just the other day. He won't interfere with you."

"You make many assumptions, Sir Edmund." The leader's face grew grave and serious as she spoke. "Dorjee Drakden will never submit to someone like you. We have known him since the dawn of time. He went by a different name then. They called him Pehar Gylapo, and he was the most feared and dangerous of all the gods. He has only ever bowed to the pure of heart, those who do not seek power."

"Huh," Sir Edmund snorted. "Don't seek power? I don't know anyone like that. Now, if we have deal, let's go."

One witch grabbed the unconscious Dr. Navel and tossed him over her shoulder like a rag doll. The group began their climb behind Frank Pfeffer, who had no idea what dangers were following him.

## 25

# WE'VE GOT
# A UNIVERSAL REMOTE
# AND WE KNOW
# HOW TO USE IT

**OLIVER EXPLAINED TO** his sister that the yak in his dream on the airplane had said *You must remember enduring Love if you want to avoid a terrible fate.* He thought he had used up the yak's prediction back with the Poison Witches.

"When the yak said *love*," Oliver told Celia, "he meant *Love at 30,000 Feet*, how I *endured* that marathon. That's why I got the message instead of you. You wouldn't have thought of it as anything you had to endure. You loved that marathon."

"It's a great show."

"Okay, whatever. Just listen. I figured once I

realized how the predication could save us back with the witches, that was it. Prophecies are sort of one-time things, right? The hero hears a mysterious message and then realizes what it means just in time to save the day and that's it."

"So now you're the hero?" Celia scoffed. "I'm the one who realized what the note really said and I'm the one that pulled us back onto the wire over the gorge."

"We're both the heroes, okay? We're both stuck, right? The point is that this prophecy from the yak wasn't, you know, disposable. I always thought it was dumb when a hero—sorry, *heroes*—got some supernatural message and could only use it once."

He took the backpack off and rummaged around in it. The *TV Guide* was soaked and what was left of the cheese puffs was squished into a weird orange mush, but he pulled out the fancy remote control.

"It's just like having a different remote for the TV and the DVD player and the stereo and you can never figure out which one goes with which thing. If you had one remote like this that worked for everything, that'd be better, right? It's the same with the yak."

"But you can never figure out what all the buttons do. How does that help with the yak?"

"If anyone could solve the riddle every time, what would be the point of sending a mysterious message? But I think I figured it out. The yak was talking about this moment too! He wanted me to remember that *Love at 30,000 Feet* marathon so we would know that the witches were showing us a fake show, but *also* because we sat still and quiet for fifty hours—"

"Fifty-two."

"Fifty-two hours. If we can do that, we can meditate. We just have to pretend we're watching television."

"We're at the bottom of a pit in a ruined shrine to a demon king, while a fake monk is looking for ancient tablets that our lost mother says don't exist, while our father is in a soul-stealing death coma. *How* are we supposed to pretend we're watching television? If I saw that on TV, I wouldn't believe it!"

"Just imagine that statue there is the TV, like a really dull public TV documentary, and, you know, watch it."

Celia sighed, but she decided to humor her brother. What choice did she have?

"I get to hold the remote, then," she said.

"But it's all wet. It's probably broken."

"Still. I get to hold it."

"But you always get to hold it," Oliver argued. "And there's not even a real TV!"

"If we're going to do your silly meditation plan, then I need to hold it so it's like normal," she explained. "When we watched the *Love at 30,000 Feet* marathon, I had the remote."

Oliver couldn't argue with her logic, so he handed over the remote, and the twins returned to their cross-legged positions.

As the light flickered on the floor behind them, the twins stared at the statue of the ferocious protector-spirit. At first, their minds were racing over their troubles again, over boring public television documentaries they'd seen in the past, over their grim future if they lost their father, if they became Sir Edmund's slaves, if they started middle school without cable TV.

"How can I tell if I'm meditating?" Celia whispered.

"I don't know," Oliver replied. "Sometimes, on TV, people hum."

"They hum?"

"They hum when they're meditating."

"What do they hum?"

"I don't know."

"I could hum the *Love at 30,000 Feet* song again."

"Anything but that!"

"Hey, you said yourself it was part of the yak's message."

"Okay, hum it." Oliver sighed. His sister was right. If the yak said it, it might be a good idea to obey. So far, the yak with the green eyes had known more about the dangers they faced than their father had.

"Hmmm Ummmm m mmm mmmmy . . . mmm's m mmm m mmmmyy," Celia hummed. "Hm mmmm um . . . hmmm mmm mmm mmm . . . hum mmm mm hum-mmmm. Hum . . . mmmm."

Oliver listened and looked at the statue. His mind wandered to the green-eyed yak. Celia was focused on the tune of the song, on turning the words into hums, on how the opening credits went.

But then, as they let the sound of the waterfall

in the distance take over, their minds started to clear. They stared with blank faces at the way the shadow of the statue in front of them danced on the wall, the way the darkness around the statue grew darker the more you stared at the brightly lit parts. They sat in the dark with their mouths slightly open, their eyes somehow wide and half closed at the same time, and their limbs hanging limp by their sides, unaware of the world around them, just like they were in the late hours of Saturday morning cartoons.

Oliver didn't notice that Celia had stopped humming. Celia didn't even notice that she had stopped humming. They were approaching a state their parents called *couch-potato-zombie brain*, but the monks of the monastery might have called it *Samadhi*—the perfect state of meditation.

It didn't help when a figure stepped from the shadows behind them and tripped over the flashlight in the middle of floor.

"Ouch!" a voice shouted. Oliver and Celia snapped out of their trance and spun to see a pile of maroon and yellow cloth, with a tiny shaved head poking out of it, facedown on the floor. "That hurt," the voice said.

"Who are you?" Celia snapped.

The face looked up quickly. It was a boy, a young monk about the same age as Oliver and Celia.

"I live here," the boy answered. "I was supposed to watch over the monastery . . . but it caught on fire, so I hid. I hoped someone would come back eventually to get me. Are you here to get me?"

"We don't even know who you are," said Celia.

"I just told you," the boy said as he stood up and brushed the dust and ash off of his bright robes. "I live here. I was supposed to be on guard, but . . . you know . . . I got distracted and the place caught on fire."

"Another monk." Celia looked nervously at her brother and raised her eyebrows.

"I'm Oliver," Oliver told the boy, extending his hand. The boy shook it. Hesitantly, Celia introduced herself too.

"Have you lived here a long time?" Oliver asked.

"Almost as long as I can remember," the boy answered. "I grew up here."

"So you would know if there were any visitors?" Oliver was excited now, and no longer annoyed that their meditation was interrupted. "Did you ever a see a woman here? One who maybe looked like us a little bit? She, ummm, well . . . she made that film projector upstairs."

"Dr. Navel!" The boy smiled. "Yes! We made that projector together. I love to build things. I helped her find some pieces for it because it's not so easy to get parts down here. She taught me English too, so I really liked her. She left the projector here for me and I was happy it didn't burn up too, though I don't have any movies for it. You are her children! Now I recognize you from the film she showed! Oliver and Celia, of course, of course. Hi! Welcome! How are you? How was the journey here? Not too hard I hope."

He spoke really fast, like he hadn't talked to anyone in a long time.

The twins looked at each other, amazed.

"Where . . . ummm . . . Where did our mother go?" Celia asked. She was nervous. Of all the clues they'd chased all over the world with their father, this was the first real one they'd ever found.

"She went to seek the source of the greatest knowledge in the world," the boy said. "Surely you knew that."

"We . . . well," Oliver said, while Celia just looked at her feet. Neither one wanted to admit that they'd never believed their mother was really still looking for the Lost Library of Alexandria. They thought she'd just run away from them.

"She won't find it, though," the boy said.

"She won't?" Oliver said. "How do you know?"

The boy just shrugged. "Can't say."

"Because it's not real?" Celia asked.

"Who can say what is real and what is not? We had ice cream here until the freezer broke. Then it melted into soup. Was it still ice cream? I ate it to find out. Then it became part of me. When was it ice cream? When was it soup? When was it me? All reality is an illusion."

"You sound like Lama Norbu," Oliver said. "And he turned out to be a total fake. His real name is Frank. He wasn't a lama at all. Or a llama. He pushed us down here."

"Oh," the boy said sadly. "So you didn't come here looking for me?"

"Well . . . no . . . ," Oliver said. "Not exactly."

The boy sighed.

"But we can take you with us, if we find a way out of here," Celia promised.

"No," the young monk said. "I think I should stay and watch over this place a while longer. I think I may have fixed the ice cream machine. I just need a few more weeks working on it. With ice cream, this place was pretty nice. But, if you wish to follow your mother's path to Shangri-La, I can show you the way."

"So Shangri-La is real?" Oliver wondered.

"Names are not important. Call it whatever you like. Find it wherever you like." He smirked at the twins. "But to continue your journey, this is the path to take."

Celia made a little twirling gesture with her finger next to her forehead and raised her eyebrows at her brother. He understood. That was the universal sign for "this-kid-is-a-total-nut."

The young monk walked up to the ferocious statue of the demon king and pressed on the statue's third eye. With a creaking sound, a doorway opened behind the statue, revealing a long dark tunnel.

"The third eye is always more useful than the other two," the boy said, and smiled.

"More tunnels," Oliver groaned.

"You should go quickly," the boy said. "The fake

lama has a head start, and your entire family remains in grave danger."

"But how did you—"

"There is no time now." The boy handed Oliver the flashlight and started to push the twins into the tunnel. "Good luck. And don't forget your bag." He gave the backpack, which now held only a wet *TV Guide* and some soggy cheese puffs, to Celia.

"What's your name?" Oliver called back as the boy shoved Celia in behind Oliver and began to close the door.

"Pehar Gylapo," he answered, and he sealed the children into the dark.

"Pehar Ghee-what?" Oliver called through the door.

"I'm sure we'll meet again," the boy shouted, his voice muffled by the heavy stone. Celia pushed on it, but it didn't move. She listened and couldn't hear a thing through it.

"He's locked us in," she said.

Now there was only one way for the twins to go and neither of them knew where it led.

## 26

# WE'VE HAD QUITE ENOUGH OF TUNNELS AND BAD GUYS

**"SERIOUSLY?" OLIVER SAID** as he began to follow the tunnel, which sloped upward and was only wide enough to go single file and only tall enough for them to sort of stand. Even in the dim light of the flashlight, Oliver could see cobwebs and the bones of strange animals strewn about.

"Why is it always tunnels? Couldn't, just one time, somebody say, 'Hey, Oliver and Celia, this way, take this well-lit and nicely carpeted hallway to the comfortable waiting room where you can wait patiently for your problems to be solved while watching TV? Huh? Noooo . . . it's always dark tunnel this and dark tunnel that. Or climb over this thing and fall down that thing."

Celia just let her brother complain while he crept along. He was, as usual, in front and groping his way forward as the slope got steeper and steeper. Complaining was his way of staying calm. Her way to stay calm was to stay angry. And right now, she was very angry.

She was angry at her mother for leaving them, for never even sending a message and then for sending a secret weird message that they might not even have been able to decode. She was angry at their father for dragging them along and then falling into a trap, for trusting Lama Norbu and Choden Thordup and not recognizing them as fakes. She was angry at Sir Edmund and at Lama Norbu, who was really Frank Pfeffer, and at the Poison Witches, for obvious reasons. She wanted nothing more than to get out of this tunnel, get her father back, and show them all that you don't mess with the Navel Twins. When this was over she would demand cable, but not *just* cable. She wanted all of the premium channels with movies and the shows that let people use curse words.

"There's nothing about adventuring that says it has to be filled with darkness and cobwebs." Oliver was still complaining to himself. "Agent Zero travels first-class on airplanes and always stays clean when he's having an adventure. There's never any bat poop. Why do we have to deal with bat poop? That's the grossest poop there is. Except maybe lizard poop. I hope we don't have to deal with lizard poop."

"Oliver?" Celia interrupted.

"What?"

"Don't you think we should focus on, you know, trying to figure out what's going on? Like, who was that Pehar Guhwhatever kid? And where are we going? And what happens when we get there?"

"Right," Oliver said.

"So . . . ummm . . . any ideas?"

"About what?"

"Any of it? The action-adventure stuff is your thing."

"You like *Agent Zero* too. I've seen you watch it."

"I like Corey Brandt, who *plays* Agent Zero. That's different. And I liked him better in *Sunset High*."

"Can we not talk about vampires while we're crawling in a dark tunnel, please?"

"Okay. So, if this were *Agent Zero*, what happens now?"

"Well, this is the impossible-escape-from-disaster part right before the big showdown with the bad guy."

"All right, but which bad guy? We've got the witches and Sir Edmund and Frank Pfeffer and the guys from the airplane and even that yeti. Who do we showdown with?"

Oliver stopped and Celia bumped into him from behind again.

"Ouch, why do you always do that?" she said.

"I don't know."

"Well, don't stop like that anymore."

"No, I mean, I don't know who we showdown with. There aren't usually this many bad guys."

"Well, there aren't usually ancient tablets and coded notes that are really film strips with Mom's handwriting on them and fake monks with fake guns and yaks giving you messages in dreams. So maybe we shouldn't go by what *usually* happens."

"Okay, then," Oliver snapped back at her. "So what doesn't *usually* happen?"

"Well, we don't *usually* end up wandering around in dark tunnels. We don't *usually* discover ancient artifacts, and we don't *usually* save the day. So, I think we should keep walking and do all three of those things."

Oliver couldn't argue. He turned and kept walking. They climbed up through the tunnel for hours. Sometimes it was flat and straight; other times it was almost like climbing a ladder.

But how were they supposed to save the day? Oliver wondered. Why did their mom go through all that effort to hide a clue in a projector that only Oliver and Celia would recognize? And what were they supposed to find if there were no tablets? How would they save their father from the witches? Why wasn't he the one out here trying to rescue them?

Their father probably wouldn't have even figured that projector out. He would have been too busy trying to read the images on the walls. Anytime there was something to read, he always picked that over watching. He didn't think you could learn anything by watching stuff. Their mother had gone off to look for the Lost Library, so they guessed she probably felt the same way. But what if they were wrong about her? What if she wanted her kids to find her? What if she had been guiding them all along?

Celia was thinking about the picture too. She was thinking about the key on her mother's necklace, the same as on the tunnel walls. It was also on the rings that the air marshal and the man in the shiny suit on the airplane were wearing. It was the same symbol that had been in the fake version of *Love at 30,000 Feet*. What was their mom trying to tell them? Why would she have the same symbol as the henchmen on the plane?

As time passed the temperature started to drop. The air got colder and colder and they started to see their breath hanging in front of them. The sweat on their skin started to freeze. They began to shiver.

"I think . . . we're really . . . high up," Oliver panted. "I think . . . we must . . . be near . . . the top . . . of a mountain. . . . On the inside."

"Don't . . . talk," Celia said. "Too . . . tired. Can't . . . take . . . another . . . step."

"Good," Oliver said. "Because we're out of steps."

Celia looked up and saw that they had reached the end of the tunnel. There was a door in front of them with a big metal handle. The door was painted with an image of the same crazy three-eyed demon whose statue they'd watched like a television down in the pit. Right in the center of its snarling demon face was that symbol again, their mother's jeweled key and the Greek words they recognized by now: *Mega biblion, mega kakon.* Big books, big evil.

Oliver swallowed hard.

"Ready?" he asked his sister as he reached up and put his hand on the door.

"Not really," she said.

"Shangri-La could be on the other side of this door," said Oliver.

"So could the witches," answered Celia.

"Mom could be on the other side of this door."

"So could Sir Edmund."

"Yeah, but—"

"Or Frank Pfeffer."

"Right, but—"

"Or the yeti."

"Okay, I get it!" Oliver said. "But we've still got to open it!"

Celia exhaled slowly and nodded to Oliver. He pushed the door open.

At first there was a blinding white light and a blast of cold air. Snow swirled into the tunnel and blocked their view. When the blinding whiteness cleared, the twins found themselves staring directly at the shining black horns and glowing green eyes of an enormous yak.

# 27

# WE'VE GOT TO TRUST THE YAK

**"KHRUUUMPF,"** the yak grunted.

"It's the talking yak from my dream!" Oliver shouted once he overcame his surprise.

"What's he saying?" Celia asked.

" 'Khruuumpf,' " Oliver said.

"What does that mean?"

"I don't know."

"Is 'khruuumpf' the sound a yak makes?"

"I don't know."

"Well, 'khruuumpf' isn't very helpful."

"I think he might only talk in dreams."

"Well, we don't have time for you to go sleep."

"I think we're supposed to ride him."

"Did he say that?"

"No." Oliver pointed. "But he's wearing a saddle."

"I can't remember," Celia said. "Do yaks eat people?"

"I hope not," Oliver answered.

"Khruuumpf," said the yak.

On the yak's back was a large saddle made of thick brightly colored carpet and leather straps. With the cold dry air blasting into the tunnel and the snow swirling around, the blanket saddle looked very inviting, even though it smelled absolutely terrible. One thing that the twins quickly learned about yaks is that they do not smell good, even the mystical green-eyed ones.

"Yaaaaarrr," the yak said, which could have been a happy noise or could have been gas.

"We have to trust the yak." Oliver held his nose and climbed on, then hoisted his sister up.

The yak turned and began walking away from the small entrance to the tunnel and up the rocky slopes of the mountain. Celia grabbed one of the blankets and wrapped it around Oliver. Then she wrapped another around herself. Sitting on the yak was surprisingly comfortable and the yak moved along the icy and rocky ground much more easily than the twins could have on foot.

"I hope he knows where he's going," Celia said.

"He hasn't been wrong so far," Oliver answered as he patted the yak's thick brown fur.

"Hey Oliver," Celia said, her voice sounding relaxed for the first time in two days. "Look at that."

Oliver turned and saw a distant mountain with a line of ants marching around it. When he looked closer, he saw that they weren't ants, but people who looked tiny next to the giant mountain, hundreds of people walking single file. Some of them held flags and banners; some of them held tall poles with spinning prayer wheels at the top. Some of them held nothing but packs on their backs, and every few steps, they would kneel on the ground and then bend down and touch their foreheads to the cold earth. A few people even stretched out like they were lying down for a nap. Then they stood up again, took a few more steps and lay down again. When the wind changed directions they could hear the crowd murmuring and chanting, though they couldn't make out any words.

Oliver looked in the other direction and saw a vast icy plain stretching into jagged mountain peaks under a bright blue sky. As they continued up, they could see behind them and down toward the gorge, a shock of tropical green below the brown and white of the high plains. Both of the twins felt light-headed from the altitude, but the yak climbed onward, upward, for hours and hours.

"Khruuumpf."

"Did the yak say something?" Celia asked.

"No," Oliver said sadly. "That was my stomach. I'm starving."

Celia just grunted. She was hungry too. They hadn't eaten since breakfast with Lama Norbu, back when he was Lama Norbu. She hoped that wherever they were going, they had some not-poisoned food. Cheeseburgers would be nice, chicken soup would be fine. Maybe some hot chocolate. She hoped it wouldn't be something slimy.

The sun was setting and the sky turned a glistening shade of orange and yellow and red over the snowcapped mountains. The ice shimmered in the last light of the day, and the cold seemed to thicken around the twins.

"It's getting really c-c-c-cold," Oliver said through chattering teeth.

"I hope we g-ge-get where we're going s—ss—sss—soon," Celia agreed.

Within seconds it was dark, a terrifying, howling-wind, ice-cold dark. The yak didn't seem to mind and just kept climbing, stepping up onto rocks and scurrying up the steep slope at impossible angles. The children wrapped their blankets tighter around themselves and held on tighter to each other.

There is a kind of tiredness that only an unlucky few ever know. It's the tiredness of ultra-long-distance drivers and of deep-undercover-special-forces soldiers, and of students who forgot to study for their history test until the night before. Celia and Oliver felt that kind of tiredness. Even though they were cold, and frightened, and the yak smelled worse than a turkey sandwich left all year at the bottom of a locker, they both fell into a deep sleep.

Oliver dreamed of his mother giving them a slide show of the years she had been missing, using the strange skeleton projector. Celia dreamed that her father was riding a yak into the Himalayan Mountains toward Shangri-La to save her from the Poison Witches while she slept peacefully in a hut with satellite TV.

With a shock, the children awoke to the sound of a gong, a really big gong. When they uncovered their faces, they saw that they were stopped inside the courtyard of a monaste /, surrounded by young monks who were all essed just like the little boy they met in the c: There were children of different ages and siz but all of them had shaved heads and wore i roon and yellow robes. Some were playing arou 1, chasing each other or making faces, but mos were standing in a circle around the yak, clappi g. The sun was high and bright overhead. The ya к was chewing comfortably on some grass that a group of young monks were feeding it.

"Where are we?" Celia asked.

"And why are all these kids clapping at us?" Oliver wondered.

"They clap to ward off evil," a voice called from a wall high above them. It came from an old man wearing a monk's robes with a giant yellow hat shaped like a crescent moon. Two giant Tibetan warriors stood on either side of him wearing large swords, heavy cloaks and grim expressions. When the old man in the big yellow hat spoke, all the children grew quiet. The gong next to him sounded again. "They clap so that you would wake and be free of the dark dreams that brought you here."

"Okay," Celia shouted up, still quite distrustful of monks. "Where is *here*?"

"You are at the Monastery of the Demon Fortress of the Oracle King," the old man said. "I am the abbot here, and I have been expecting you. I'm very glad you survived the waterfall and found your way to us. Come inside and have a bite to eat before we get down to business, as they say." He glanced quickly at the guards next to him and Oliver thought the old abbot looked frightened.

"What do we do?" Oliver wondered.

"Eat, I guess," said Celia as they hopped off the yak.

From the shadows of an upper window, a figure watched the twins follow the abbot and the large warriors inside. Just as Celia glanced up, it disappeared from view. She wasn't sure if she even saw anything at all.

"Something's not right about this place," she said to no one in particular. She had no idea how true that was.

# 28

# WE SHARE A DISAPPOINTING DINNER

**THEY ENTERED A GRAND** room with a giant U-shaped table in the middle of it. The walls of the room were hung with painted silk that showed stories from the history of Tibet. There was even an unfinished image that looked like it was the Hidden Falls with the three rainbows in front of it.

The table was set with wooden bowls and platters, bronze and bone cups and plates. Over a hundred young monks were seated around the table and they were chatting loudly. When the abbot entered the room with the twins, all their heads turned toward them and the room fell silent.

"We are a monastery devoted to finding the next generation of sacred oracles," the abbot explained. "All of our students are studying the Buddhist arts of divination. That is how we came to expect your visit. I, myself, had a vision of your arrival."

He gestured for Oliver and Celia to sit with him at the head of the table. There was a giant curtain behind them that made Oliver feel like they were on a stage, like they were actors in a big show.

After a moment, all the monks started talking to each other again. It didn't feel like a stage anymore. It felt like a school cafeteria, with all the murmuring and the curious glances toward the twins. Kids at school glanced at them like that too, whenever they returned from some exotic country covered in bites from exotic lizards.

"Why do people keep looking at us?" Celia asked. She did not trust monks after Lama Norbu had turned on them. The boy from the cave seemed all right, though. He had gotten them out after all.

"We do not get many visitors here," the abbot said. "We are hidden from the rest of the world."

"Is this Shangri-La?" Oliver asked.

"All will be made clear to you," said the abbot. He glanced nervously at the two large warriors standing right behind him. The abbot was making Celia nervous. "First, you should eat," he added.

A gong sounded and servants appeared carrying giant iron pots. The abbot said a blessing and then all the young monks grabbed at plates covered in something like flour and dropped them into their steaming cups of butter tea, swirling the mixture until it became a wet paste. Then they grabbed the wet paste into clumps and popped the clumps into their mouths. Servants poured noodles and vegetables from the iron pots into wooden bowls, and the whole room filled with the sounds of slurping and sipping. Celia smiled widely. She was starving and hadn't seen any fried bugs being served.

Suddenly, the servants appeared beside Oliver and Celia and set out steaming plates of noodles with bubbling blobs of meat.

"Just for you," the abbot said. "White sheep's tail. We are, of course, vegetarians here, but you are growing and need your strength. The tail of the white sheep is a special delicacy."

The pinkish blobs of meat glistened in the sunlight. Celia squirmed. Oliver started to reach for the plate, because he was hungry, but Celia elbowed him under the table.

"If you eat it, then I have to eat it," she said. "And I am *not* eating it."

"You have no sense of adventure," Oliver said.

"You sound like Dad," answered Celia, and Oliver blushed. He hated to think he was turning into someone who liked adventures.

"Of course, if you prefer, we have steamed vegetables, noodles, barley flour, and dried yak's tongue," the abbot interrupted, trying to make the twins more comfortable.

Oliver's eyes went wide thinking of the yak who had saved their lives. His stomach did a backflip. Certainly they wouldn't cook a mystical yak.

Nope, he thought, I am not turning into someone who likes adventures at all.

"Where's your sense of adventure now?" Celia laughed. She thought how her parents would have loved this, sitting in a weird monastery on a mountaintop, watching everyone eat gooey butter-tea bread balls. The sounds of sipping and slurping made her stomach grumble.

"I told you." She elbowed Oliver again. "I told you on the plane that this is exactly what would happen."

"You said bugs," Oliver snapped back. "You said we'd have to eat bugs. And there's no bugs."

"Curried yak's eye?" the abbot offered gently, gesturing toward a bowl of reddish liquid with little slimy balls the size of marbles floating in it. Both children's faces turned green. Celia had gone eleven years without eating an eyeball and she planned to keep it that way. Oliver just froze. He almost wished for bugs.

The abbot did not want to make his guests ill. He had two more bowls of noodles and vegetables placed in front of them and he waved the bubbling sheep's tail, sizzling yak tongue, and steaming eye-curry away. The two warriors behind him immediately snatched it all from the servants and devoured the steaming meat with their bare hands. The abbot looked at the warriors with wide eyes.

"Something's not right here," Celia whispered.

"I know," said Oliver. "Keep eating, though. Don't make them suspicious."

The twins focused on the noodles and soups and even tried dropping the flour into their tea to make little wet bread balls the way the other monks were doing.

It felt amazing pouring the warm food into their stomachs. The noodles were thick and hot and the broth was rich and soothing. Even the butter-tea bread balls were tasty and salty and filling.

"I could win *Celebrity Whisk Warriors* with this stuff," Oliver said.

"You've never cooked anything in your life." Celia laughed. This was the first rest they'd had in ages and for a minute they forgot about their mother and father and their long list of worries.

But they didn't forget for long.

After only a few minutes, the abbot smiled and rose. The monks around the table fell silent again and stood up. Oliver and Celia stood too, even though they weren't done eating, because they didn't want to be the only ones not standing. The abbot seemed in a hurry.

"When in Somalia," their father used to tell them, "do as the Somalis do." The twins assumed the same lesson was true for Tibet.

"Now that you have eaten," the abbot said, "I must talk to you about the important matters that brought you here."

The twins looked at each other, wondering how much he knew.

"I am afraid," the abbot said, "that you are in much more trouble than you know."

"Well, we know that our father made a bet with Sir Edmund about the Lost Tablets of Alexandria, and that the Poison Witches took our father to try to get them, and that we are lost on a mountain in the middle of nowhere in Tibet."

"You are not nowhere," the abbot corrected her kindly. "You are at the home of the sacred oracle. As for the other matters you mention, they are unfortunate." The abbot sighed. "The witches are treacherous, but they can always be bargained with. They do love to trade."

"We were supposed to trade the Lost Tablets with them."

"I am afraid that will be impossible. There are no tablets."

"We know," Oliver objected. "But it's the only way to save our father! Our mother's note sent us here. The yak brought us here. Even that kid— Pehar something—helped us get here! There has to have been some point to it!"

Celia wanted to shush her brother, but she also wanted to hear what the abbot had to say.

"*Who* helped you?" the abbot asked, his face suddenly looking alarmed and glancing quickly at the large men behind him. Celia didn't like it when a monk's face looked alarmed. The last time that happened, Frank Pfeffer revealed his treacherous plans.

"Pehar Ghee-lap something," Oliver said.

"Pehar Gylapo?"

"Yes," Celia said. "That was it. That's the kid we met in the cave."

"We met him in the cave behind the Hidden Falls," Oliver explained. "And he showed us the way to get here."

"That is quite impossible."

"That's what he said," Celia huffed.

"Why would we lie?" Oliver pouted.

"Well, children." The abbot bent down to their level. His face showed great concern. His voice dropped to a whisper. "Pehar Gylapo is the Great Protector of Tibet. If what you say is true . . . if the Great Protector has chosen to help you, there may be hope yet. I will pray for you, but right now, I can do no more than that."

"Um . . . why's that?" Celia asked.

"Because of us!" a voice shouted, and the giant curtain behind them rose up into the ceiling. The twins spun around, startled.

There behind them, seated on a throne beneath a giant statue with many arms, was Sir Edmund, surrounded by a crowd of serious-looking men.

"They arrived while I was away," the abbot said, standing up again. "They took control of the monastery and the oracle. I had no choice but to help them. I am sorry."

"Welcome, Navels," Sir Edmund hissed. He stood on his throne to look more intimidating. "So nice to see you again."

"I've seen this sort of thing in a movie before," Celia whispered. "It doesn't go well for the good guys."

"Well, I guess this is our showdown," Oliver answered as all the monks rushed out of the dining hall and more large, heavy warriors marched in.

"I guess it is," said Celia, because she liked to get the last word in.

Oliver just hoped it wasn't her last word ever.

# 29

# WE WONDER WHAT CELIA'S UP TO

**SOME OF THE MEN** around Sir Edmund wore the robes of Buddhist monks, others were in the black robes of priests, and some wore business suits. There was even a man in blue jeans and a T-shirt, with a baseball cap pulled low over his face. They all wore medallions around their necks with the image of a scroll locked in chains.

The abbot stepped back, mouthing another apology at the twins. He didn't wear a watch, but he tapped his wrist and ran right out of that great room like he was late for an appointment. Two very large Tibetan guards wearing swords on their backs blocked the doorway after he left, so that the twins could not escape.

"I am impressed," Sir Edmund said. "I did not expect you to survive this long on your own, nor did

I believe you would make it here. I had expected someone else to walk through those doors."

"Lama Norbu's not even a lama," Oliver said.

"No?" Sir Edmund laughed. "So you figured that one out, eh? The great Frank Pfeffer couldn't even hide himself from Oliver and Celia Navel? Pathetic."

"We know you were in cahoots with him," Celia said defiantly. She'd heard the word *cahoots* on *Animal Detectives*. She thought it sounded like the kind of word that explained what criminals did. "We know you threw us out of the airplane and sent that yeti after us and got the Poison Witches to take our father!"

Some of the other members of the Council shifted uncomfortably.

The man in the T-shirt and baseball cap shouted "Aha!" and started typing a text message into his cell phone. Sir Edmund glared at him and he stopped texting.

"Well," Sir Edmund said. "You are much more clever than I had thought. I am guilty as charged. The plan with the witches was to poison *you* and force your father to lead us here. The witches' foolishness changed those plans, but you have done admirably in your father's place. Though I must tell you that I didn't have anything to do with throwing you out of the airplane."

"You didn't throw us from the plane?" Oliver muttered, confused. "If you didn't get us thrown from the airplane, then who did?"

"I don't think you want to know," Sir Edmund said, and the entire Council chuckled.

"Where's our father?" Celia demanded.

"He is safe for now. For one more day, at least."

*"Where is he?!"* she yelled.

"My, oh, my. No need to shout, child. You really want to know?" Sir Edmund waved to one of the guards, who pushed aside the curtain over the room's only window. In the distance, there was a jagged mountain peak, even higher than the mountain peak they were now on. "He is camping with the witches on top of the sacred mountain. Mortals fear to trespass on its slopes, so I promise you they will not be disturbed. In fact, I've placed plenty of guards around the mountain to make sure of it. And your old friend the yeti is up there too. She's looking for her child, the baby yeti I captured, I imagine. I think that has put her in a bad mood. So if you have any ideas about rescuing your father, I would quickly forget them."

"What do you want from us?" Oliver said. "There are no Lost Tablets."

"I know there are no Lost Tablets, boy," Sir Edmund snapped. "I destroyed them myself!" He shook his head and looked a Celia. "Was your brother dropped on his head as a child? Too much music television maybe?"

"We don't have music television," Oliver objected. "We don't even have cable."

"Children," Sir Edmund sighed. "You aren't making this very easy for me."

"Let our father go," Celia said, "and then we'll do whatever you want. We'll tell you what our mother's note means. We'll tell you everything we know."

"You will?" Sir Edmund said.

"We will?" Oliver whispered at his sister.

Celia didn't even look at her brother. She was trying her best to stare down Sir Edmund and hoping he wouldn't notice that she was lying through her teeth.

# 30

# WE DIDN'T PLAN FOR THE PLANE

"**WE FIGURED OUT THE** clues in our mother's note," Celia said, when the room fell totally silent. "We know all kinds of secrets. Now give us our father back or we won't tell you anything!"

No one said a word.

Oliver looked from his sister to Sir Edmund and back to his sister again. She set her jaw tight. She was grinding her teeth, which she only did when she was really nervous. The room stayed deathly silent.

"Yeah!" Oliver finally shouted, more to break the tension than anything else.

"Oh, children," Sir Edmund said, and sighed loudly. "Didn't your parents ever teach you not to lie?"

"We're not lying," Oliver said, trying to defend

his sister. He was pretty sure she was lying, though. She wouldn't have figured out all kinds of secrets from their mother's note and not told him, would she have?

Sir Edmund just shook his head and blew air out through his teeth. He sounded like a balloon deflating, and even from several feet away the twins recoiled at the smell of his breath. Even the other Council members looked uncomfortable.

"Unfortunately for you, there is absolutely nothing I want from you," Sir Edmund said at last. "There is nothing you can tell me or give me that I need. This is as close to Shangri-La as anyplace on earth, and there is no Lost Library here. There are no tablets. Right now, you are completely useless to me."

All eyes in the room went back to Celia. Even Oliver was speechless.

"But . . . if you aren't looking for anything . . . ," Celia stammered. "Then why . . ."

"Why go through all this?" Sir Edmund said. "Because we *are* looking for something. Or rather, someone. your mother. We imprisoned the Oracle of Dorjee Drakden, but he wouldn't tell us where your mother was. We couldn't understand your mother's clues in that note, but we very much wanted to find her after all these years. You see, while there are no Lost Tablets, I believe that she copied them before the Council was able to destroy them all. She has the only copy of the Catalog of the Lost Library."

"You did all this for a library catalog?" Celia exclaimed.

"Oh, yes," said Sir Edmund. "With that catalog, we would be very close to finding the Lost Library itself—all the knowledge in the world would be under our control. All that power! We couldn't have your mother finding it and putting it in a museum, now, could we? We must find it first. We must destroy her copy."

Celia couldn't believe all this was happening. Everything had been a lie. This wasn't about discovering something at all. It was about destroying their mother's discoveries.

"I thought there was no better way to bring your mother out from wherever she was hiding than to put her family in danger. I was amazed she didn't appear when you were attacked by the yeti. I was amazed she didn't help with the Poison Witches or the waterfalls or Frank Pfeffer. I'm beginning to wonder if I made a mistake, if maybe your mother just doesn't care about you at all."

The twins said nothing. They were starting to wonder too.

"That yeti seems to care more for her monstrous child than your mother does for you. I'm not surprised, I suppose. Such dull children you are. I can't blame her for throwing you out of the plane."

"What was that?" Celia demanded.

"Oh, you hadn't figured that out yet?" Sir Edmund replied casually. "It seems like something from one of your soap operas, doesn't it?" He smiled, enjoying himself. "She's the one who had you thrown from the airplane."

# 31

# WE WISH THIS WAS
# A BETTER STORY

**OLIVER AND CELIA** couldn't believe it. They stood in silence thinking about their mother and the key symbol and the plane and everything they'd been through.

Sir Edmund nodded at the guards. They grabbed Oliver and Celia from behind and lifted the kids off their feet.

"You're a liar!" Celia shouted. Who could imagine her own mother tossing her out of an airplane?

Sir Edmund didn't answer. He just kept smiling. The guards started to drag Oliver and Celia from the room. Celia had seen enough Spanish soap operas to know that if your family was insulted, you had to defend their honor, no matter what. And her family's honor had been insulted enough for one day. She reached back with her free arm and pulled one guard's giant curved sword from its sheath. The blade sparked as she pulled it free, and the startled guard released her. She spun to face him and waved the sword to make him back up. The other guards drew their own swords and circled around Celia.

"Sis, what're you doing?" Oliver called out, still held firmly by his guard.

"I'm setting us free," Celia answered.

"Is this like the pushing thing again?"

"A little bit," Celia answered, spinning slowly with her sword raised, trying to watch the crowd around her.

"I think it's going to work about as well," Oliver said as the guards closed in on her. She swiped at one group, who leaped backwards as another group of guards lunged at her from behind. She ducked and kicked and blocked the way she'd seen Señorita Solano do on *Amores Enchiladas*. Sparks flew as their blades met, but the guards were wearing her out quickly. Hours and hours of watching romantic sword fights can teach a person technique, but it is hard to build strength sitting on the sofa. And no one sweats on soap operas. Celia's hands were slippery.

One of the guards rushed at her with his sword raised high, ready to swipe down and split her in two. She lifted her sword to block him, and, at that moment, another guard grabbed her from behind around the waist and lifted her into the air. Her sword slipped from her hand. The fight was over.

Sir Edmund clapped.

"Thank you so much, young lady," he said. "That was entertaining. But I think we've had enough."

With that, the guards dragged Oliver and Celia kicking and screaming from the room. One of them snatched Oliver's backpack with a violent yank, nearly ripping out his shoulders. Celia bit her guard's hand, but he didn't seem to mind.

"I didn't know you could fight like that," Oliver said as they were pulled along.

"Me neither," panted Celia, still out of breath.

They reached a heavy wooden door with a big lock on it. A prison cell. The room had no windows or other doors. There were no statues with third eyes to press, or corners where strange monk-children could hide to come to their rescue. The guards tossed the twins into the room like rag dolls and slammed the door behind them. They heard locks and bolts slamming shut.

"This is bad," Celia said.

"That wasn't much of a showdown," Oliver agreed. "We mostly got beaten up and locked away."

"Well, it's not like we've had much help. Our only friends so far have been a yak and a strange kid who might have been a spirit or just a weirdo living in a cave."

"You really think Mom had us thrown out of the airplane? Why would she do that?"

"She had that symbol on her necklace in the picture, the same ring that the air marshal and the man in the shiny suit had."

"And the people on the fake *Love at 30,000 Feet*. What do you think it means?"

"I don't know," said Celia. "I just don't know. I can't figure all this out. How am I supposed to figure everything out? I'm only three minutes and forty-two seconds older! I can't do everything!" She was crying now. "I'm not like Mom and Dad at all. I'm not a genius or brave or adventurous. I'm just not."

"Calm down." Oliver hugged his sister. "It's okay. It'll be okay."

"You don't know that," she sniffled.

"Yeah I do."

"How?" She wiped the tears out of her eyes.

"Because," said Oliver. "At the end, when things look the worst, there's always a turnaround. It's a rule, just like the wire breaking. This is just how things happen. It's just good storytelling."

Oliver knew a lot about good storytelling. You can't watch as much television as he did and not learn a thing or two.

"Not on *Love at 30,000 Feet*," Celia sniffled. "That show's been on forever, and things always get worse. The Duchess in Business Class doesn't even know that Captain Sinclair is hiding his deep vein thrombosis."

"That's that thing you get if you sit too long on an airplane?"

"Yeah."

"I always thought it was some kind of musical instrument."

"Well it's not. It's a serious medical problem. And the captain has it."

"Well, *Love at 30,000 Feet* is different," Oliver explained. "But trust me, in stories about kids in trouble, there's always hope."

Celia sighed. Her brother was right. If this was

anything like TV, there had to be a happy ending. It was about time for their adventures to be more like TV. So far things were not going at all like they should.

"All right," she said at last. "We're going to make our own happy ending."

"Okay."

"Okay."

"Good."

"Yes."

"Okay."

"Here we go."

Minutes passed in silence.

"Celia?" Oliver said after five minutes in the dark without a word or a sound.

"Yeah?"

"You aren't doing anything."

"I thought you were."

"What was I supposed to do?"

"I don't know. I just figured you'd do something. You know, all that good storytelling and happy ending stuff."

"I was trying to make you feel better."

"So we still don't have any way out of here?"

"No." Oliver thought for a minute. "Wanna try meditating again?"

"Absolutely not."

"Yeah, me neither."

They sat in silence again. It was hard to tell how much time had passed in that little room with no windows.

"Why did that yak lead us here?" Oliver wondered after a while. "Why did Mom's picture show us this place if we were just going to be betrayed by that old abbot? If Sir Edmund was telling the truth, then Mom's trying to kill us too!"

"We were better off in the cave with that kid," Celia agreed.

Suddenly, a loud gong sounded right outside their door. There was a moment of quiet and then it sounded again, louder.

*BONG!*

Everything was silent and then they heard the click and squeal of the bolt sliding back. The door opened and the room was flooded with light. The two guards were unconscious on the ground and the old abbot was standing above them holding a big gong. He smiled when he saw the children.

"I find that sometimes the sound of the gong alone is not enough to chase away evil," he said. Then he stepped aside. A nun stood behind him covered in robes, her head bowed. She held their backpack out and Celia took it from her.

"Thanks," she said.

"You're welcome, Celia," the nun said, dropping the robes from her head and looking up. She had long dark hair and big dark eyes, and she was not a nun at all.

"Mom!" both children gasped.

"We have very little time," said their mother.

# 32

# WE ARE FAMILY

**"I AM SORRY I BROUGHT YOU HERE,"** their mother told them quickly. "But it was the only way. I am proud you made it this far, but you still have farther to go."

They could already hear guards coming around the corner toward them. There was no time for hugs or questions or tears. The monastery was usually a quiet place. The sound of two loud gong strikes and two bodies hitting the floor had certainly been noticed. The abbot dragged the unconscious guards into the cell, tossed the gong on top of them and shut the door.

"You go," the abbot said. "I will delay them. It is the least I can do for bringing such misfortune to your family."

Their mother nodded at him, then grabbed Oliver and Celia's hands and rushed with them down the hall. They slipped behind the door to the nuns' quarters just as they heard loud voices shouting at the abbot. Their mother stopped a moment to listen.

"What was that noise?" one of the guards demanded.

"It must have been a loud television," the abbot explained.

"There's no television here!" the guard shouted.

"Oh, some of our monks have a weakness for the soap operas, *The Lovers at 10,000 Meters* and whatnot. It's really quite a fine—" The abbot couldn't finish his bogus explanation. A guard thumped him on the head and locked him in the cell.

"This way," Dr. Navel told her children.

"What's going on, Mom?" Oliver asked.

"I can't explain right now, Ollie," she said. "I promise I will. But right now, we have to run, before things get really dangerous."

"They already are really dangerous!" Celia whisper-shouted. "Sir Edmund said you had us thrown out of the airplane!"

"That was for your own safety. If you had landed in the capital, you would have fallen right into Sir Edmund's hands."

"But we fell into his hands anyway!" Celia yelled. "And we could have died!" Her shouts echoed through the halls of the monastery.

"Honey, I know you're mad," their mother said, looking around nervously. "But believe me, things will get a whole lot worse if we don't go right now."

Without waiting for Celia to reply, she half dragged, half pushed them through a maze of hallways and chambers. Monks and nuns poked their heads out of doors and watched the Navels rush past. They all seemed to know Oliver and Celia's mother; they all wanted to help. As they rushed, Oliver and Celia heard shouting from down the hall. Nuns were arguing with guards.

"We will go where we please," they heard Sir Edmund shout. "On the authority of the Council, let us pass! Ouch!"

Someone had hit him with a cooking pot.

"Here we are," their mother said, stopping in front of a high window. The view looked out over a snowy plain, hundreds of feet below. In the distance, they saw the mountain where their father was held.

"This way," Sir Edmund was shouting. "Those

kids can't have found this place alone. They have help. I know it!"

Worry spread across their mother's face, but she hid it quickly.

"We have to climb out on the ledge," she said, stepping up onto the windowsill and pushing open the glass.

"What?" Celia shouted, not even bothering to whisper-shout. "You disappear for three years, have us thrown out of an airplane, and now you want us to step out on a ledge thousands of feet in the air? We are only here because of you! Because of you and that stupid library."

"She's just angry," Oliver said, not wanting to hear his mother yelled at the first time he saw her in years, "because whenever we climb anything, we end up falling. I mean, really falling really far . . . like out of an airplane."

"I'm sorry, guys. Excitement's still not your thing, is it? Well"—she looked at Celia—"this time you won't fall."

"Why not?" Celia crossed her arms and leaned back on her heels. She was in full-on stubborn mode.

"Because I've got you," their mother said as she

reached down and pulled Oliver up onto the ledge next to her. He didn't resist. If felt good to be with his mom.

"Come on, Celia," he said. "I'll go first. Like always."

They heard the clanking of boots coming toward them. Doors burst open. Nuns screamed and clapped. The sound was getting closer.

"Fine," Celia said, and let her mother help her up to the ledge. "But you carry the backpack." Their mother agreed and took it, not even asking what was inside.

They stepped out onto the ledge and knocked the window shut behind them, slipping to the side just as the door burst open.

"No one here," Sir Edmund shouted, looking into the room. "Next." He and the guards continued on, while Celia and Oliver pressed their backs hard against the outside wall. The ledge was slippery and every time their weight shifted, they slipped a little bit. The wind pushed at them like a bulldozer and their mother put her hands across their chests, helping them stay back. Down below them on the ground was a large cage with a heavy wooden door that led back into the monastery. In it, exposed to all the wind and the cold, a yeti paced back and forth. It looked right up at Oliver and Celia and roared.

"A yeti!" Oliver yelped, remembering his last encounter all too well. This one was smaller than the one that had attacked him, but still looked ferocious.

"It's just a baby," Dr. Navel explained. "They brought it here a few days ago. It hasn't stopped pacing since they took its mother away." She grew quiet for a moment. "Okay, stay close to the wall," she said at last, changing the subject. "Put your feet down carefully in front of you. Don't shift your weight onto a foot until you've set it firmly. You don't want to slip on the ice. We're just going around the corner ahead of us. Fifteen feet. That's all."

Their mother was going first. Oliver held her belt with one hand and used the other one for balance. Celia held on to him the same way. And they started forward together without another word. It was the longest fifteen feet of their lives. If they survived it, Celia thought, their mother had a lot of questions to answer: three years, a yak and an airplane's worth of questions.

# 33

# WE VISIT AN OLD FRIEND

**THEIR MOTHER REACHED** the corner first. She disappeared around the edge. For a moment Oliver and Celia were alone again, slipping and sliding on the narrow ledge, freezing and shivering hundreds of feet in the air. Then her hand shot back around the corner.

"Okay," she called out. They couldn't see her face, but they could hear her. "One at a time I want you to jump straight out and grab my hand!"

"What?!" Oliver shouted back.

"JUMP AND GRAB!" their mother yelled. Oliver looked back at his sister.

"*I* followed *you* out here," she said.

Oliver took a deep breath and pushed off from the wall, jumping toward his mother's hand and the open air. He caught her by the wrist and she tightened her grip around his. She used the forward motion of his jump to swing him around the corner, his feet flying out through the sky behind him. And she kept swinging him, right up above herself, right over the top of her head.

"Whoaaa!" he yelled. When he was above his mother, looking straight down at her and the ground way below, she let go of his hand. He kept going up in the direction she swung him, and found himself flying through an open window one floor up. He flew through feetfirst and landed on a pile of books, maps and papers, which scattered around him.

The room was dim. There was only a small lantern glowing on wooden table. He stood up and walked over to the table. He could hear his mother shouting at Celia outside.

"Just trust me!" she was yelling.

"Why should I trust you now?" Celia was shouting back.

"Because we have to get off this ledge!"

Oliver looked at the table. It was covered in scraps of paper with notes and sketches on them just like the one Choden Thordup/Janice McDermott had brought to the Explorers Club. In the corner of the room there was a mat with a pillow on it. This must be where their mother was hiding. Right under Sir Edmund's nose. The room didn't seem to have a door. Was that why their mother had to toss them in?

Suddenly, Celia came spinning through the window with her feet over her head and landed in a heap on the pile of books. The backpack flew in after her.

"Oliver!" they heard their mother calling. "Celia!"

They went over to the window and looked down at their mother.

"I'm going to jump and, if you can," she shouted, "please catch my wrists and pull me in so I don't fall. Then, I promise, you can be mad at me."

Oliver and Celia looked at each other and sighed. Then they reached their arms out and caught their mother's hands when she jumped up. They strained to haul her up into the room. The yeti looked up at them, licked his lips and bared his massive fangs. When their mother was inside at last, Oliver and Celia stepped back away from her, panting to catch their breath.

The twins and their mother stood for what felt

like forever staring at each other. Their mother was lit from behind and her dark hair seemed to glow with the light from the window. After all this time, she didn't even seem real, but there she was. She had a few more wrinkles on the edges of her eyes and the corners of her mouth than last time they saw her, but otherwise, she looked the same. Her eyebrows were raised in that curious expression she had, one that Celia often made too. Celia used it to show her annoyance, where her mother used it with a kind of eagerness, a welcoming look that said wordlessly "What's next?"

"Should I hug you?" their mother asked. "I want to hug you. I know you're mad, but I'm your mother and I really want to hug you."

"Not yet," Celia added, still angry. "First tell us what's going on."

"I can't," Dr. Navel said. "It's better if you don't hear it from me."

"No!" Celia yelled. "I've had enough of that. No more deciding what's better for us and what isn't. Dad says it's better for us if we don't watch too much TV, if we get out and see the world. Well, the world has nearly gotten us killed and all that television is the only thing that's kept us alive so far! So you tell us and *we'll* decide what's better for us. We're not kids anymore, like when you left. We're eleven now. Did you know that? We turned nine while you were gone. And then ten, and you still weren't back. Now we're eleven and you have to tell us why you were gone so long and why we had to almost die to get you to come find us!"

Their mother just looked at Celia for a long time. She looked a little sad, but also a little happy, the way people look when they listen to violins.

Oliver and Celia shifted uncomfortably in the silence. They heard the high mountain wind whistling outside.

"You have grown up a lot," their mother said at last. "But I meant that it is better if you hear it from him."

She pointed behind them and both children turned. Standing in front of them was a monk dressed in elaborate robes and armor with a sword shimmering in the dim light.

"Oliver, Celia," their mother said. "I'd like to introduce you to my friend Dorjee Drakden, oracle, warrior-god and Consul General for the Great Protector Pehar Gylapo."

The spirit suddenly filled the monk's body and he let out a loud hiss. His chest puffed and he slashed his sword through the air, spinning and coming toward them. Oliver and Celia drew closer to each other. The oracle stopped in front of them and spoke in the voice of Dorjee Drakden.

"The greatest explorers shall be the least," he chanted. "The old ways shall come to nothing, while new visions reveal everything. All that is known will be unknown and what was lost will be found." His face had turned red and agitated. He paused and then added. *"Trust no one!"*

"Um," Celia said. "What was *that* about?"

"That was a prophecy," Oliver said.

"How do you know?"

"Because that's what prophecies sound like. They're cryptic."

"What does *that* mean?"

"It means, 'having a meaning that is mysterious or obscure,' " Oliver said. "At least, that's what the yak told me."

"That was why I brought you guys here," their

mother said. "To hear that prophecy. It is *your* prophecy."

"But why?" Oliver demanded. "Why us? We don't even like to leave the couch!"

"Because it is your destiny to find the Lost Library," their mother said.

Suddenly, the oracle spun around the room waving his sword, hissing and panting. He knocked all the papers from the desk and tipped over a small chair. The little monk seemed barely in control of his body, like the spirit was trying to break free of him. Finally, he stopped in front of Oliver and Celia again. He raised his sword above them and gripped it with both hands, like he was going to chop them apart. And then he pulled a universal remote control out of his sleeve. It was the one they'd left in the cave with the boy.

"For you," the oracle said, in a totally different voice, almost like a child's. "All fixed." He hissed again, right into their faces, and crumpled to the floor in a pile of robes. "Told you we'd meet again." He winked and then fell sound asleep. The spirit had left his body.

Oliver stood looking at the remote, wondering how it could have gotten here from the cave.

"I'm sorry," their mother said. "I tried to protect you for so long."

"Yeah, great job," Celia said.

"I did what I could. I made that note that only you would understand to try to get you here without the Council knowing why. Dorjee Drakden and I did what we could with the airplane and the yak. We even made that fake version of your soap opera, Celia, because I knew you would recognize that it was fake. It's hard even for Pehar Gylapo to broadcast images mystically like that, and he's the most powerful spirit in these mountains. It took a lot of convincing, but I thought it might save you from the Poison Witches. I'm sorry it didn't work in time to save your father, but mystical television programming is not as easy as it looks."

"Who is this Council?" Oliver wanted to know.

"They're also looking for the Lost Library. They have been for thousands of years. They want all of its treasures so they can rule the world. For the last three years, I've been trying to beat them to it."

"But why bring us now, though?" Celia demanded. "Why after all this time?"

"Because of the prophecy you just heard," she said. "Because it means that I cannot find the library myself; only you can find it. I wanted to spare you. I thought I could find it without you, but I couldn't. You are the only ones who can uncover its true location."

"In Shangri-La?" Oliver asked.

"Some might call it that," she said. "Others might call it Atlantis or El Dorado or the City of Z. It's a blank spot on the map. Every time in history has such a place. Shangri-La is just one of them. But there are others, lost places where lost things go."

"How are we supposed to find *that*?" Celia asked. "Why do people keep expecting us to find things? We're not explorers! What are we supposed to do?"

"You have all the tools you need. I've kept it from Sir Edmund and his Council all this time—a perfect copy of the Lost Tablets."

"We have that?"

"I hope you do," a voice said from behind them.

Frank Pfeffer climbed up from a trapdoor in the floor, pointing his gun at the Navel family. "Because you're going to give it to me. And I can't wait to announce the discovery myself at a very large press conference! Where the Navel family failed, Frank Pfeffer succeeded! The Lost Library of Alexandria! Should I announce it in Beijing? New York? Los Angeles? Perhaps there's a movie deal in it for me. . . . Oh, and before you get any ideas," he added, "I assure you, the bullets in the gun are quite real this time."

# 34

# WE VISIT A NEW FRIEND

"**YOU'LL NEVER WIN**," their mother said. "I didn't tell you anything in the Gobi Desert; I won't now."

"You made me look like a fool."

"I did what I had to do."

"And you will again. You will give me this copy you mentioned, or I will shoot one of your children. Which should it be?" He lowered the gun to Oliver and Celia's level and moved the barrel back and forth. "Eeny, meeny, miny, moe, catch a Navel by the toe," he chanted.

"Is this the happy ending you mentioned?" Celia whispered to her brother.

"Wait!" Oliver said. "We'll help you."

"What?" their mother said.

"What?" Celia said.

"What?" Frank Pfeffer said.

"We'll give you what we have. We don't care about all this Lost Library stuff. It's just a bunch of books." He looked over at his mother sadly. "We just want our mom back."

Frank Pfeffer smirked.

"But you can't kill us later," Celia added angrily. "Bad guys do that kind of thing all the time."

"Deal. Though it won't be much help for your father with those witches," he said, and laughed.

"You snake, you lousy, scheming . . ." Celia searched for the right word to yell at him. *"Charlatan!"*

Frank Pfeffer just laughed. "We're running out of time for name-calling, little girl. Why don't you just give me what you've got now?"

"No," Dr. Navel said. "It's too important." She was pleading with her children.

"Here you go," Oliver said, ignoring his mother. He dropped the remote control into his backpack and pulled out the collar he'd taken from the yeti.

"What is that?" Frank Pfeffer said.

"It is the Great Key of Alexander," Oliver said.

Celia and his mother looked at him like he was crazy.

"What does it open?" Frank was practically panting.

"The Catalog Room of the Great Library," Oliver said. "The room is the size of a circus tent, with thousands of scrolls telling you all its mysteries." He winked at his mother and sister.

"The Lost Tablets," said Frank Pfeffer.

"Yeah," said Oliver. "They existed all along . . . right here in Shangri-La."

"You will not make me look like a fool again," Frank said.

"Why would I lie now? You've got the gun."

"All right then, Oliver. Lead the way."

Oliver slipped carefully down the trapdoor. His mother followed. Celia was at the back with Frank, who held her by her collar and kept his rifle pointed at their mother's back.

"No funny business," he said.

"Trust me," Oliver said. "I don't want to be funny."

They climbed down the ladder into a dark hallway. They pressed themselves flat against the wall when they heard guards rushing down the hallway.

They streaked past, all clattering swords and flapping robes. The man in the baseball cap led them.

"You go that way," the man shouted. "And you lot, that way. Find them! Go!" The guards ran off in opposite directions. Oliver waved their little group forward and they continued to a winding stairwell.

"I think it's this way," he said. Celia wondered what her brother was doing, but if she'd learned anything in the last three days, it was that she should probably just trust him. They'd kept each other from dying so far.

"What are you doing, Ollie?" Dr. Navel whispered.

Oliver ignored her. He led them down a narrow hallway to a heavy wooden door on the outside wall.

"This is it," Oliver said.

"Good," said Frank Pfeffer. "Now give me the key."

"You'll need to show it to the guardian of the room, in order to get past," Oliver explained, handing him the collar.

"No, Oliver," Celia added. "Don't give it to him!" She'd realized what her brother was up to.

"Give that to me," Frank said, snatching the collar from Oliver's hand. "Oh! I am about to become the most famous explorer in the world. Too bad your father won't survive to see this. Maybe I'll get your apartment at the Explorers Club." He laughed and opened the door right into the baby yeti's cage.

"ROOOOAAAR!" the yeti growled as it stood up straight, at least twice the height of Frank Pfeffer.

"Bow to the Key of Alexander," Frank shouted.

The yeti cocked its head to the side for a moment, confused. He looked at the explorer and he looked at his mother's collar in the man's hands. He cocked his head to the other side. Then he saw the rifle.

"ROOOOAAAR!" he said again and knocked the gun from Frank's hand with a single swipe.

"Ahhhh!" Frank said, and turned to run, but Oliver and Celia slammed the door on him. They rushed away toward the exit to the courtyard. They didn't want to stick around and hear what the yeti did to the man it thought had taken his mother.

........................................................

"Good thinking, guys," Dr. Navel said to her kids.

"You're a real Agent Zero," Celia told Oliver, and she meant it this time. Oliver blushed a little bit.

"The yeti just misses his mother," Oliver explained. There was a long silence while Oliver and Celia looked at *their* mother.

"So what did you mean we have everything we need?" Celia asked at last.

"Shhhh," their mother said.

They crouched down as another group of guards rushed past, led by Sir Edmund. Once the group had gone, she gestured for Oliver and Celia to follow her. They got out to the courtyard, where their yak was still tied up.

"You have to go to the mountain and get your father," Dr. Navel said.

"What about you?" Celia asked.

"I am going to lead the Council away from you."

"But you can't just leave again," Oliver said.

"I promise, one day, I will be back."

"But what about the prophecy and stuff?"

"Trust me, guys. Don't freak out. I love you

very much. Just remember to always be yourselves and you'll be okay. You know far more than you think you do. When the time is right, you'll find me again. For now, just try to get home and watch some TV. And don't let Sir Edmund get his hands on the catalog."

"But we don't even know—"

She cut Oliver off with a tight hug and kiss on the top of his head. Though Celia resisted a moment, she did the same to her and Celia melted into her mother's smell of perfume and shampoo and dirty yak fur.

"What do we do about the witches?" Celia said at last. "Without the Lost Tablets, how will we get Dad?"

"Just remember what you know," Dr. Navel started to say. "They can't make—"

"Hey!" The shout came from above. It was Sir Edmund standing with a phalanx of guards on a stone balcony. "Stop them!" he shouted.

"Good-bye, kiddos," Oliver and Celia's mom said as she set them on the yak and whacked it on the behind. The yak took off toward the slopes of the mountain in the distance. Oliver and Celia looked back as their mother raced off on foot in the opposite direction, pursued by large Tibetan warriors.

As their yak raced upward over gnarly rocks and frozen scrub, they saw the guards only a few feet from their mother. She had stopped at the edge of the gorge, which dropped off thousands of feet below. She turned around and pulled a leather journal from under her robes.

"Is this what you want?" she shouted. "My copy of the Lost Tablets?" The guards froze. She waved the book in the air a few times. Then she gave one look back at her kids riding to safety, and tossed the book into the air. The pages flew apart and scattered in the wind.

"Noooo!" Sir Edmund shouted as the guards scrambled to catch the loose paper. Dr. Navel laughed and took one big leap out into the void.

"Mom!" the twins shouted, but a moment later, they saw her sailing along the edge of the canyon, gripping tightly to the wings of a small glider.

"Stop her!" Sir Edmund shouted as he raced down from the monastery and sprinted across the icy ground, snatching and jumping at loose papers as he ran. Though the warriors tried shooting arrows and firing their rifles at Oliver and Celia's mother, they couldn't even come close. She was rising like a hawk on the wind and in only a few minutes, she was gone. As the yak moved farther and farther from the monastery, they heard Sir Edmund shouting at his guards.

"You fools! The papers were blank! It was a trick. Go after her! I can't believe you fell for that!" His voice faded into the distance. The twins were alone again and their father was running out of time.

# 35

# WE CAN'T COOK EITHER

**THE YAK KNEW WHERE** it was going. It didn't hesitate and it didn't look back. All Oliver and Celia could think about was hesitating and looking back. The last few hours felt like a dream. Had they really just seen their mother? Had she really just left them again?

The yak shot up the mountain as fast as a . . . well . . . a really fast yak. There's nothing that really compares to a yak running at tremendous speed. Except maybe an out-of-control bulldozer covered in fur.

"What do you think she meant," Celia shouted, "when she said the witches can't make something? What can't they make?"

"I don't know!" Oliver shouted.

When they arrived at the edge of the mountain, the sun was just beginning to set. It was the fifth day. If they didn't get to the witches soon, their father would be lost forever. The yak stopped. It wasn't going any farther. Oliver tried to yank it, to keep it going up, but an eleven-year-old who sits in front of the TV all day has little chance of moving a two-ton yak that has just run a marathon. Oliver had never run a marathon. Neither had Celia. The yak's expression told them that it was not easy.

The children had to go on foot. Celia let Oliver carry the backpack.

"Thanks," he said sarcastically.

"I'll go first," Celia said.

"You will?"

"Yeah. I'm better at stealth than you."

"Since when?" Oliver demanded just as he tripped over a knobby root sticking out of the ground.

She's protecting me again, Oliver thought, kind of annoyed. And kind of grateful. He really didn't want to go first. Those witches scared him.

The twins scrambled over rocks and leaped between boulders. They ducked behind a bush when they saw a group of the council's large guards pass on horseback. The men were huge. They carried shining swords and were dressed like warriors from another time, some time long ago when people didn't hesitate to slice children in half with their shining swords.

They climbed as quickly as they could over rocks and ice. When they came to the witches' camp inside a cave of ice, they ducked behind a boulder and watched the witches in the reflections off the ice. They were reflected back over and over again at crazy angles. It was like being in a funhouse.

The witches had set up their huts in the same circle they had in the valley. They had even set up the satellite dish. They sat around a campfire, cooking. Dr. Navel lay unconscious on the ground next to the fire. He was snoring quietly. Every few seconds, he would groan.

"At least Dad's still warm," Celia said.

"He's almost out of time."

"What do we do?"

They listened in on the witches.

"Put in more butter! That's too much salt!" the leader shouted at the one stirring a big pot.

"Don't tell me how to cook. Everything you make tastes like wood."

"I wish what you made tasted like wood!" she

snapped back. "I don't even want to say what your food tastes like."

"Say it, I dare you."

"Or what?"

"You'll regret it."

"The only thing I regret is letting you make dinner!"

"Gimme that *TV Guide*," Celia whispered. "We'll make a trade for something even better than the Lost Tablets of Alexandria."

With that, she stood up and waved the *TV Guide* in the air.

"Yoo-hoo!" she shouted out. "Ladies! We're back!"

The witches stood up, startled.

"Hey!" they shouted, looking in every direction at the reflections around them. Celia was reflected over and over again on the ice, like she was on a thousand different TV screens.

"Which one is she?" one of the witches cried out.

"We all live in a yellow submarine!" sang the musical witch.

"Hush up," the leader with the turquoise head-band snapped. "Navels! So good to see you again. I am happy that strange man you were with didn't manage to kill you. We never liked him. In truth, we have never been too fond of explorers."

"You could have told us who he really was," Oliver said, standing. He liked the way the ice reflected him over and over again. It was the first time in days he had seen himself. He and his sister were really dirty. You never see it on TV, but adventuring is a messy business, and adventurers don't smell so great either.

"Well, that wouldn't have been any fun," the leader answered.

"I wanna rock and roll all night! And party ever-y day!" the singing witch sang.

"You see what kind of entertainment we're stuck with?" the leader said.

"That's why we're here," Celia added. "We're willing to make a trade with you."

"But there are no Lost Tablets of Alexandria. That was our deal."

"We'll make a better trade," Celia said. "You're bored? What I have here"—she held up the *TV Guide*—"is a Lost Tablet of Entertainment!"

The witches gasped, and leaned in toward the walls of ice, looking at the *TV Guide*. Corey Brandt was on the cover, peering over the top of his Agent Zero sunglasses.

"What is this magic?"

"This is a list of everything that is, was, and *will be* on television. This will tell you where to find *Love at 30,000 Feet*—for real. You can read plot summaries, you can read interviews with the stars." She looked at the witch who liked music. "There's also music television. Twenty-four hours of music videos."

"Rock and roll all night?" the witch sang quietly. The leader rolled her eyes.

"Yeah," Oliver said, grabbing the *TV Guide* from his sister. "And"—he spoke to the leader— "there are cooking shows. So many cooking shows. You could learn how to make deadly yak soufflé. Poison marinated snake casserole. Toxic beetle barbecue. The possibilities are endless. *Celebrity Whisk Warriors. Ten Ton Taco Challenge.*"

"I like tacos," the leader said.

"Aren't you tired of the same old recipes? The same old yak butter stew." He waved the *TV Guide* in the air. "Corey Brandt shares his favorite desserts."

"*Sunset High,*" the witches murmured. Even

witches in Tibet had crushes on Corey Brandt as a vampire. It was Oliver's turn to roll his eyes.

The leader thought a moment. She tapped her foot on the ground. She looked back at her companions, who nodded eagerly at her. "One moment please." She gathered the witches around her in a huddle. They chatted and whispered and screeched and consulted.

"Ladies," Celia said, pointing at her father on the ground. "We're running out of time over here."

Finally, the leader turned around and puffed her chest out like she was about to give a long speech.

"Okay," was all she said, and she nodded. One of the witches went over to Dr. Navel and fed him a greenish liquid from a small clay pot. He coughed and his eyes fluttered. Oliver and Celia stepped out from their hiding places and came into the clearing. Oliver handed over the *TV Guide*, and the witch opened it, her eyes wide.

"*Cooking with Carl*," she read excitedly. "*An All-Day Meat-a-thon!*"

"Oooh . . . Meat-a-thon!" The other witches rushed to her and gathered around as they walked off into a thick mist.

"Celia . . . Oliver?" their father croaked, sitting up. His voice was scratchy and his head seemed to float on his neck, like he was dizzy.

"We're here, Dad," Celia said, rushing to him. "We're okay."

"You're alive," Oliver explained. "The witches like cooking shows."

His father smiled up at him with no idea what his son meant or where, exactly, they were.

"We'll explain later," Celia said, hugging him. She pulled back and looked him in the eyes. "Once we get cable."

Their father laughed, but his laughter didn't last long. His jaw dropped and his face went pale again. For a second Celia thought that their father was about to pass out, that the witches had lied, but she followed his gaze around and saw Sir Edmund and the rest of the Council surrounded by guards. They blocked the entrance to the cave.

"You've still lost the bet," Sir Edmund said. "There are no tablets, and therefore, you will give up the title of Explorer-in-Residence and your children will become my slaves. Accounts will be settled at the Ceremony of Discovery."

He snapped and there was a roar, a rumbling,

and a thwomping sound as the wind whipped in all directions. Snow swirled around the cave and the earth shook, like a demon was about to break free from the ice.

Instead, a large cargo helicopter with two spinning rotors popped up from below and hovered alongside the mountain. Its back hatch opened, settling onto the ground, and the Council, the guards and Sir Edmund climbed aboard.

"SEE YOU BACK AT THE CLUB!" Sir Edmund shouted over the roar of the helicopter. "THIS IS FAR FROM OVER!"

With that, the helicopter closed its hatch and peeled off into the night.

Oliver, Celia and their father were alone on the side of the mountain, high in the Himalayas.

Well, not entirely alone.

A mother yeti stood to her full height on a boulder right above the Navels and roared. "Sorry I shot at you!" Oliver called out.

"Shhhh!" Celia snapped.

"It's okay, guys," their father said. "I'll show you how it's done."

# 36

# WE DON'T DO "DERRING-DO"

Professor Rasmali-Greenberg declared that the Ceremony of Discovery would take place a month later. Everyone was excited to hear the Navels' tale of courage, danger and derring-do, which is just another way of saying courage.

Celia never understood why explorers had to use such weird words, and ever since getting back from Tibet, she had been spending more time with explorers than ever. For the past month, explorers had been pouring into the apartment on the 4½th floor asking Oliver and Celia to "debrief" them, which is just another way of saying "tell them."

"What was it like to meet the Oracle of Dorjee Drakden?" they asked.

"How did you survive the Poison Witches?" they begged.

"Did you really feed Frank Pfeffer to a yak?" they winced.

Oliver had to explain over and over that the oracle was just a kid, except when he was a crazy hissing monk, and that the Poison Witches just wanted some new recipes, and that no, Frank Pfeffer was not eaten by a yak. "Yaks don't eat people."

"Oh," all the explorers said, disappointed.

"It was a yeti," Oliver corrected, and the explorers brightened. Celia rolled her eyes at her brother. It looked like he enjoyed telling the story, like it was something that happened on television to some other kids. Like it had been fun.

"You're turning into an explorer, you know," she said.

"Am not."

"Are too."

"Am not."

"Are too."

"Am not!"

"Are too plus infinity."

Celia always got him with that one.

"But how did you escape the yeti?" the explorers begged to know. "Why didn't she eat *you*?!"

"We will have a full debriefing at the ceremony tonight!" Professor Rasmali-Greenberg interrupted. "The children will tell you all you want to know about their brave escape from the yeti and how they came to lose the wager with Sir Edmund. But for now, please leave them to watch their television in peace."

He smiled at the twins as he ushered all the explorers off the 4½th floor. Oliver and Celia were finally alone.

"What's on?" Oliver said, turning back to their brand-new TV. It was a big flat-screen and it had simply been there when they got back. It even had a bow on the top of it, but there was no note telling them who gave it to them. They had barely turned it off since getting home, even though they still didn't have cable. Their father didn't want to install cable if he was getting kicked out of the club in a few hours for losing the bet with Sir Edmund. The twins knew that they would have to surrender to Sir Edmund at the same time, and become his slaves for the rest of the summer. That was *not* going to happen.

They were going to run away for real this time.

They hadn't told anyone about the prophecy and they didn't want to. If anyone believed that they were destined to become great explorers, they'd never be left alone. Their father would make them search the world looking for clues and Sir Edmund would chase them to who-knows-where to find the Lost Library and whatever time they didn't spend on mountain peaks or in the deep sea, they would spend "debriefing" people. They'd never have time to watch TV again.

That's why they planned to run away later that night. A new backpack was packed with clothes and snacks and a fresh issue of *TV Guide.* But they didn't want to leave before they knew what would happen to their dad. His part of losing the bet with Sir Edmund was losing the title of Explorer-in-Residence and getting kicked out of the club. Oliver and Celia didn't want to leave before they knew where he would be living. They'd have to check in on him from time to time, of course. He was their father, after all.

"We'll leave after the Ceremony of Discovery," Celia said, even though she didn't want to go. She knew they would have to tell everyone how they escaped from the angry yeti. But it would be worth it to know that their dad was okay. As usual, Oliver agreed.

Just as they settled in to their last hours in front of the TV, Professor Rasmali-Greenberg and their father burst back into the apartment.

"I understand if you still want to demand answers from the airline, but I fear you will not get anywhere," Professor Rasmali-Greenberg was explaining to a frustrated Dr. Navel. "I promise I am on your side, but consider the facts, Ogden. If your wife arranged for your mid-flight departure, pursuing the matter might only put her in danger. And if this Council is as powerful as your children claim, they will certainly be working to cover everything up anyway. You realize, of course, that Sir Edmund has denied everything. And Choden Thordup has vanished. I can't believe she was really Janice McDermott. The disguise was perfect. Now I am left with no proof and a large green statue of a toothpick. I cannot go around calling Sir Edmund a liar without evidence."

"And why not?" Celia interrupted their conversation. She pressed mute on the TV.

"Hey," Oliver snapped at his sister. "I was watching that!"

She had only pressed the mute button because they were watching an *Agent Zero* rerun that she didn't care about. It was the one where Agent Zero has to escape from a floating casino that was really a nuclear submarine. Oliver watched without sound while Corey Brandt slid upside down across a wire connected to the shore. The sub was rapidly sinking and he was in danger of being dragged under into the dark waters of the Aegean Sea.

"It's gonna break," Oliver told the TV, and just like that, the wire snapped and the camera zoomed in on Corey Brandt's face looking surprised. "Told ya," Oliver said, and then turned to listen to Professor Rasmali-Greenberg answering Celia.

"I understand your anger, Celia," the professor said warmly, "especially after what you say Sir Edmund put you through in Tibet, but there are larger concerns here. You cannot begin to understand the pressures that prevent me from taking action even if I know what is right and what is true."

"Pressures!" Celia exclaimed. "Pressures!! Have you ever been thrown out of an airplane and fallen over a waterfall and been chased by angry warriors and Poison Witches and rescued by weirdo gods disguised as little monk children?! Have you?!"

"Well, actually, dear, one time, I—"

The professor was interrupted by a knock on the door. Professor Eckhart and his monkey had come to tell them that they were expected at the cocktail hour before the ceremony.

"Sir Edmund," Professor Eckhart explained, "is beginning to brag that Dr. Navel is too much of a . . . ahem . . . coward to attend." His monkey screeched.

"I'll show him a coward," Dr. Navel said, rolling up the sleeves on his tuxedo like he was ready for a fight.

"Be patient, Ogden," Professor Rasmali-Greenberg said. "And trust me. Come, Navel family! We have a ceremony to endure!"

"We're gonna stay and watch a little more," Celia said. Their father didn't argue. The twins did not want to stand around with a lot of explorers more than they had to.

Once they were alone, Oliver snatched the remote back from his sister and turned the sound on.

"I want to watch something else," Celia said.

"You don't even know how to use the remote," Oliver argued.

"Neither do you," she objected.

"Do too," Oliver said, and started pressing buttons. The screen kept changing. Different menus appeared and disappeared. Celia tried to grab it from him, while Oliver kept hitting buttons blindly and trying to keep it from his sister.

"Give it," she said, and grappled with him.

"Let go," he said as he struggled under her.

Suddenly, the screen went black and an image of a key appeared.

"Hey," Celia said. "That's—"

"—the symbol from Mom."

The twins stopped wrestling.

A new menu screen showed up.

PLEASE CHOOSE YOUR LANGUAGE, it said.

Oliver selected English and the screen changed again. It was a list, like a list of TV shows, but they had strange names like *A treatise on the process of Alchemy* and *Prophecies of Dorjee Drakden, Volume 1*.

"What is this?" Oliver said.

"I don't know," Celia replied.

"It looks like the TV Guide Channel."

"Sort of. But that key symbol."

"Oh, no," Celia said.

"Oh, no," Oliver said. He pressed the button that said INFO in big red letters.

WELCOME TO TABLET 2.0, the screen read. THE COMPLETE CATALOG OF THE GREAT LIBRARY OF ALEXANDRIA.

"Um," said Oliver. "Mom slipped us the Catalog of the Lost Library."

"She said there were no tablets," Celia said.

"This isn't a tablet," Oliver answered. "It's digital. So she didn't lie exactly."

"But . . . but . . ." Celia objected. "Why would she do this?"

"Because of the prophecy. She told us we had a copy."

"But, um . . . No! No! No!" Celia couldn't think of anything to say, but she really felt like letting the world know that she was not happy about this.

"What do we do?" Oliver finally asked.

"Watch something else!" Celia demanded. "I don't want to get involved in this. I don't want to eat eyeballs or ride yaks or fall off anything anymore!"

Oliver turned the TV off.

"If we show this at the ceremony," Celia added, "we could win the bet. It's a copy of the Lost Tablets."

"But then Sir Edmund and his Council would have it. Mom told us not to let it fall into his hands. If we hand it over, everything we went through would be for nothing. And, you know, Sir Edmund's Council might take over the world."

This was why their mother wanted them to keep watching TV. This was how they were supposed to find the Lost Library in whatever lost land it was hiding. But another adventure was the last thing they wanted. Oliver hadn't been bitten by an exotic lizard in months, and he was going to keep it that way. Whatever clues lurked in that remote control, he did not care to look for them. At the same time, they couldn't just turn it over to Sir Edmund.

"So we'll have to keep it a secret," Celia agreed. "You aren't very good at secrets."

"Am too," Oliver said.

"Are not."

"Am too."

"Fine. You are," Celia gave up. "Let's go to the ceremony and get this over with."

When she turned to go, Oliver dropped the remote control into their getaway backpack. You never know when a universal remote that opens up the only copy of the Lost Tablets of Alexandria would come in handy.

# 37

# WE'RE AT OUR LAST CEREMONY

**THE COCKTAIL PARTY** before the Ceremony of Discovery was under way when they arrived. The usual cast of explorers, adventurers, scientists and globe-trekkers were talking and drinking and telling stories to each other about their latest adventures.

As Oliver and Celia walked in, the room fell silent and everyone turned to look at them. Celia felt as if the eyes of the stuffed animals on the walls were following her. Oliver gripped her hand. Their father rushed over from where he'd been talking to Madame Xpertina, the motocross rider, and hugged them both.

"So glad you have chosen to join us," Sir Edmund called from the stage at the far end of the room. He was wearing a tuxedo but had pinned tons of medals and ribbons to it, awards he had received or bought from governments and armies all over the world. Some of them even looked like antiques. He couldn't possibly have earned all those medals, Oliver thought. As they drew closer, they saw that his cufflinks bore the symbol of the scroll wrapped in chains, the symbol of the Council.

"I am a man of my word," Dr. Navel told him, mounting the stage and taking the attention from Oliver and Celia.

"Good, then we'll begin!" Sir Edmund tapped one of his medals on the edge of his sherry glass, making a loud ringing sound. "Attention, all! Attention!" he called out.

"Excuse me, Sir Edmund," Professor Rasmali-Greenberg interrupted. "I believe I will call this meeting to order. I am, after all, still the president of our esteemed club."

"Of course." Sir Edmund smiled and bowed a little too dramatically, like he was making fun of the professor.

"Ladies and gentlemen," Professor Rasmali-Greenberg called out. "Honored guests. Tonight is a very special ceremony. Not for a long time have we had such momentous events on which to report. Our own Explorer-in-Residence, Dr. Ogden Navel, is recently returned from Tibet. As you have certainly heard, it was a journey of great importance and even greater discovery. A wager was made and tonight, we shall settle the results."

Dr. Navel looked sadly at his children, who looked angrily at Sir Edmund, who smirked with smug satisfaction.

"The wager concerned the Lost Tablets of Alexandria," Professor Rasmali-Greenberg continued. "These tablets, as we have learned, were not found. Nor, it seems, was the land of Shangri-La. Given the terms of the wager made at this very ceremony earlier in the summer, the bet is won by Edmund S. Titheltorpe-Schmidt the Third."

The room ignited with chatter. Explorers gasped and muttered. Some traded dollar bills and gold coins from side bets they had made with each other about who would win. Some of them clinked glasses and toasted Sir Edmund. Oliver saw that there were other people in the room who wore the symbol of the scroll locked in chains. Those were the only people cheering Sir Edmund's victory, but there were several of them. Maybe that was why the professor couldn't accuse Sir Edmund of anything. Maybe he had too much support from his mysterious Council *inside* the Explorers Club.

"You see that?" Celia whispered to Oliver.

"I see it," he said. "We can't let them find out about the remote control that—"

"Shhhh," Celia cut him off. "Don't talk about it! *Secret*, remember!"

"Oh, right."

"Silence, please!" shouted Professor Rasmali-Greenberg. "As is our tradition, we shall read the terms of the wager."

Professor Eckhart's monkey climbed onto the stage, carrying a giant old book bound in thick leather and stitched with gold lettering. Every bet that had ever been made at a Ceremony of Discovery was written in its pages. The monkey handed it to Professor Rasmali-Greenberg, who flipped through it and scanned up the pages with his finger.

"Nosferatu . . . Necromancers . . . ah! Navels!" he read. "Per the terms of the wager, upon failure to find the Lost Tablets of Alexandria, Dr. Ogden Navel shall be banished from the Explorers Club in disgrace forever and his children—that's you"— he looked at Oliver and Celia Navel—"shall surrender themselves to Sir Edmund S. Thitheltorpe-Schmidt the Third for every vacation from school no matter how long, be it for summer, or a holiday, or a teacher's conference, or a temporary building evacuation because of lead paint toxins, until they turn eighteen."

The room was silent when he finished reading.

"Lead paint?" Celia whispered.

"It's a big problem in older buildings," Oliver answered. "I saw a *Newsline Undercover* report about it."

People looked at the floor and the walls. No one wanted to make eye contact with the Navel family.

"I have determined," Professor Rasmali-Greenberg said at last, "that it is within my power as president of the Explorers Club to change the terms of this wager." He handed the book back to the little monkey.

"What?" Sir Edmund shouted.

"What?" Dr. Navel asked.

"What?" said Oliver and Celia.

"Our club is one of discovery and exploration, and Dr. Ogden Navel, though he has failed to find the Lost Tablets of Alexandria, discovered much in his time in Tibet. He has firsthand experience of the *Dugmas*, those legendary Poison Witches. He has found not one, but two yetis, and he has climbed on the slopes of the sacred mountain. His discoveries, as usual, will bring honor and glory to our club. I will not expel such an explorer because of a silly bet."

"Silly!" Sir Edmund huffed.

"He must, of course, tell us at last how he came to escape the yeti on that deadly mountaintop in Tibet and how he came to return safely to us with his children."

"Gladly," Dr. Navel said. "You see, the yeti wanted to be reunited with her child, who was still in a cage down at the monastery where Oliver and Celia had left him with Frank Pfeffer."

Everyone in the room looked back at Oliver and Celia with wonder and with dread. They were the first eleven-year-olds in the history of the Explorers Club to have fed a grave robber to a baby abominable snowman.

"As Edmund certainly knows, yetis are very protective of their children and, at first, she did not want to listen to reason," Dr. Navel continued. "I tried to explain the situation, but she leaped down from her high boulder and knocked me nearly ten yards through the air. I hit my head again but, having missed so much of my children's adventures up to that point, was determined not to miss any more excitement."

"Excitement!" Celia groaned. "Was that supposed to be *exciting*?"

Dr. Navel kept going with his story. "I stood again and asked, politely, if the she-yeti would please just be patient. I asked in several languages. I even tried the universal language of interpretive dance, but she did not appear to enjoy my performance. She charged for Oliver and Celia. It was at that point that the parent in me overtook the scientist, and I threw the biggest chunk of ice I could at the beast. It hit her in the head. She froze with her giant claw raised above my children. 'Leave them alone!' I shouted. I did another dance that made my displeasure very clear. At that point, she charged at me again. After that, well, my children should tell the rest. It was their heroism that saved us all. Oliver, Celia, please come up on stage."

Oliver and Celia groaned, but they did as they were told. They wanted to get it over with as quickly as they could.

"Well . . . um . . . the mother yeti was pretty upset," Celia said. Why did all these people want to hear the story, she wondered. It was just a bunch of terrible stuff and boring adventures they'd survived. "She was going to kill our dad and probably us, so we, you know . . . ran over and jumped on her back."

"I had some experience riding her, you see," Oliver interrupted, a little excited to be in front of so many people. This is what it must feel like to be famous, he thought. Not bad. "We held on while she tossed and twisted and tried to get us off. She swatted me away and Celia started to hit her on her head. She tossed Celia off too, and all of us were scattered. She ran toward Dad, I think to eat him first. He had the most meat on him."

"That's gross," Celia interrupted.

"You want to tell it better, then?"

"Yes," Celia said. "It was right then that I remembered *Pack Masters*."

"I love that show!" Professor Rasmali-Greenberg cheered all of a sudden, and then sat quietly in his seat on the stage. "It's very educational . . ." he muttered into his hand.

"Yeah," Celia said. "So I remembered that Pack

Master Michael always says you have to establish dominance to become the Pack Master or else your dogs will run wild."

"And *I* remembered," Oliver said, "that the yeti was not a dog." It felt good to be the one correcting his sister for a change. She just glared at him and kept going with her story.

"I stood up tall between my dad and the yeti and raised my hand and said, 'No! Bad yeti!' I used the voice I use when Oliver is trying to change the channel off of *Love at 30,000 Feet*. That stopped the yeti in her tracks."

Some of the explorers chuckled. Oliver looked down at his sneakers.

"Then my brother came running over next to me," Celia said, "and he stood in between me and the yeti."

Oliver looked up again and smiled. "I shouted, '*We are the Pack Masters*!' The yeti stood totally still. The stuff really works!"

"I told you it was a good show," Professor Rasmali-Greenberg added.

Celia kept going: "I think that's when the yeti saw that we're just like her, a family that wanted to look after each other. She stopped attacking.

Then I remembered what Sir Edmund said at the banquet before we left for Tibet . . . how the yeti like musical theater. So we performed the only thing we both knew: the theme song from *Love at 30,000 Feet*."

"She must have liked soap operas," Oliver said, "because she didn't eat us. She grabbed us right up like it was nothing, one in each arm. I can tell you that a bear hug is nothing like a yeti hug. I thought Celia's eyes might pop out of her head and that the noodles I ate for lunch would pop out of my stomach. She had Dad get on her back and she sped us down the mountain, back to our yak. The yak was scared at first, but yaks are braver than people, and more trusting, so the yak just went along with us back to the monastery. The guards saw us coming and ran off. No one wants to get in a fight with an angry ycti and an angry yak, not even armed guards. We set free the abbot and the little monk who was the Oracle of Dorjee Drakden. The spirit didn't appear again, though. The little monk just thanked us and promised he'd send many blessings."

"Of course, Frank Pfeffer was nowhere to be found," Dr. Navel took over again. "We cannot be sure what became of him." He coughed, though everyone knew what had become of him. Unlike yaks, yetis were *not* vegetarians. "Anyway, you have never seen such joy as when we opened that cage and the mother and child yeti were reunited. Even our trusty yak seemed to shed a tear at the sight."

All the explorers laughed. Yaks were not known to be sentimental.

"It's normal," Celia interrupted. "We brought their family back together. Nobody likes to lose their mother." She glared angrily at Sir Edmund.

"Yeah," Oliver said, not noticing his sister's anger. He was really into telling their story. He felt heroic. "The baby yeti hugged us too, just as hard as his mother did. I thought he might squeeze us to death, but he didn't. He just wanted to play. His mother roared and he put us down. Then both of them jumped right out of the window and raced off into the snow because they were so happy to have escaped from Sir Edmund and his nasty Council."

"*Lies!*" Sir Edmund shouted, while some of the other explorers wearing the symbol of the scroll in chains pulled out their cell phones and started sending angry text messages. "This is nonsense. Children could not survive an attack from an abominable snowman! And this so-called *Council* is a fantasy. Something from one of their cable television shows!"

"Snow*woman*," Celia corrected him angrily.

"We don't even have cable and you know it!" Oliver added.

"I demand justice!" Sir Edmund shouted. "We had a wager! The Navels lost it! I demand my victory! I will not suffer these lies!"

"Calm down, Edmund," Professor Rasmali-Greenberg answered him, and turned back to the entire room. "I have decided on the second of the terms of the wager, concerning the children Oliver and Celia Navel. The wager stands."

Many people in the room gasped.

"They shall surrender themselves into the service of Sir Edmund for the rest of the summer and return to his employment every vacation until they graduate from high school."

"But he and his Council tried to kill us!" Oliver shouted. "More than once!"

"Nonsense!" Sir Edmund responded. "The boy

has watched too many spy movies! Television rots your brain, you know."

"Liar," Oliver yelled, and tried to lunge at Sir Edmund. Celia grabbed his arm and held him back.

"Such a brat." Sir Edmund laughed. "Now I understand why your mother decided to disappear."

Celia let go of her brother and kicked Sir Edmund right in the shin.

"Ouch!" he shouted as he fell.

She grabbed Oliver and pulled him off the stage, running toward the exit.

"We're running away now?" Oliver asked.

"Yes!" Celia shouted as they burst into the hallway.

# 38

# WE ARE NOT THE KEY

**THEY RUSHED PAST THE OLD** portraits of explorers, up the narrow staircase under the old flags and banners from the club's past expeditions. They sprinted all the way up four and a half flights of stairs and burst into their apartment. Oliver grabbed the backpack from its hiding place in the tunnel and Celia took a quick look around.

"At least we know where Dad will be," she said.

"What if Mom comes back?" Oliver wondered. Celia didn't have an answer to that. She just stood there silently. "Shouldn't we look for her?"

"No, we shouldn't," Celia finally said. "She only found us again so we could find the Lost Library for her! And that's the last thing I want to do. I'm done with adventures for good. And I am not going to be slave to Sir Edmund or his Council. Come on."

Oliver climbed into the tunnel ahead of his sister. He had his doubts, but he couldn't let his sister run away alone, and he didn't want to stay behind to be Sir Edmund's slave by himself. As they crawled away, they heard the door to their apartment burst open.

"Where are those brats?" Sir Edmund shouted.

"Oliver? Celia?" their father called out, worried.

Within a few minutes they had popped out of the tunnel into the library. They stood behind the big statue dedicated to Frank Pfeffer and Janice McDermott.

"Ugh," Oliver said. "I don't want to ever see that thing again."

"Okay," Celia said. "So we're going to leave this room and run right for the door. Don't stop for anything. Ready?"

"Yeah, I'm ready."

"Going somewhere?" a voice called out to them. They turned and saw Professor Rasmali-Greenberg sitting in one of the high-backed chairs facing the fireplace.

The professor stood slowly, setting down a small leather book. "I fear that the story of two children running away to seek their freedom only ends happily on television. In real life, I think you'll find that you shall meet a terrible fate on your own."

"More terrible than becoming slaves to Sir Edmund?" Celia snapped.

"Sir Edmund will never let you escape," the professor responded, shaking his head sadly.

"You could have done something to help us," Celia said. "You could have changed the bet like you did for Dad."

"I suppose I could have, Celia. But I did not."

"Why not?" Oliver demanded.

"Well," the professor said. He sighed and gestured for the children to sit down. Neither of them moved. "Okay, fine. Stand if you like." He leaned on the armrest of the chair. "I have not been honest with you for quite some time. You see, I know about the Council and I know what your mother gave you in Tibet."

"You know?" Oliver asked. "How do you know that?"

He smiled and lifted his hand. He wore a ring on his finger that had a symbol of a key on it.

"Your mother would be very proud you didn't betray her to win the bet," he said. "And now we need you."

"Who needs us?" Oliver asked. "What is that symbol?"

"It is the symbol of the Mnemones."

"What?" Oliver said. "What the heck are the Knee-Moans?"

"The Mnemones were the scribes in the Great Library of Alexandria. Whenever a ship came into port, all its books would be taken and copied by the scribes. Whenever a new land was conquered or a new discovery made, the Mnemones were the first to learn about it and to study it. They recorded all of the knowledge in the world. They wrote the tablets.

"But the leaders of Alexandria didn't want anyone but themselves having all that knowledge. So they decided to destroy the Mnemones and their records. In the battles that followed, the library itself burned down. The books and treasures were feared lost. But they were not lost. They were hidden. Your mother has spent the past three years trying to find out where.

The Council is searching too, and they will stop at nothing to get their hands on it. Your mother stayed away all this time to keep you safe from them. But then she heard that prophecy from the oracle. She knows that she is not the one who is destined to find the library. You two are."

"No," Celia said.

"I don't want to be a Knee-Moan," Oliver said.

"We're not going to find anything. We're going to run away now, like we should have done before."

"You can't run from your destiny."

"We can try," Celia said.

"A wise poet once said that one often meets one's destiny on the path one took to avoid it."

"What's that supposed to mean?"

The professor just shrugged. "If you do stay and fulfill your part of the wager, when you return from your summer job with Sir Edmund, you will have *all* the premium channels. Not just basic cable. Everything. Everything you could ever want to watch."

"Everything?"

"Nature. Movies. Cooking. Soaps. The Travel Channel. Everything," the professor said.

"No travel," Oliver said. Celia just crossed her arms in front of her chest. She was angry that this had been hidden from them. The Council and the Mnemones and their mother were all part of some ancient treasure hunt, and Oliver and Celia were supposed to solve it for them? That was crazy. They just wanted to be left alone.

"You don't have to find anything," the professor continued. "All I ask of you is that you honor your father's bet with Sir Edmund and work for him. Who knows? You might learn something useful. You might accidentally *discover* something, in which case, I would appreciate if you wrote it down and told me about it when you got back." He smiled kindly. "Just like scribes."

"Or spies," Oliver said, a little excited.

"You want us to spy on Sir Edmund," said Celia flatly.

"I do," said the professor. "And after what he did to you, I would imagine you might want to spy on him also."

"We just want to be left alone," Celia said.

"Well, my young friend, I do not need to be an oracle to tell you that that is not going to happen. Your life is going to be an adventure whether you want it to or not. You have a choice, however, over what you do with that adventure. I suggest you take advantage of it. No matter what, you are going to have to endure it."

Just then the door to the library burst open and Sir Edmund, Dr. Navel and a crowd of explorers burst in.

"There they are!" Sir Edmund shouted.

"Ah, Sir Edmund, good to see you," the professor said. "The children are packed and ready, as you can see. I was just giving them some parting advice." He smiled at them. "And some reading."

He handed Celia the small leather book from his chair. She looked down at the spine. It was engraved with a symbol of a key.

**A HISTORY OF THE GREAT SCRIBES OF ALEXANDRIA,** the spine said in gold lettering. **BY CLAIRE S. NAVEL, PHD.**

"Mom," Celia whispered.

He handed Oliver a small leather book as well. This one didn't have a key symbol on it. Just a picture of a llama.

"A llama?" Oliver complained. *"A Guide to*

*South American Flora and Fauna*?" he read. "By Dr. Ogden Navel, PhD. What's flora and fauna?"

"It means plants and animals," Dr. Navel said, smiling. "I wrote that book the year you were born."

"Why not just say plants and animals, then?"

"Because they're explorers," Celia said. "That's why."

"I trust you will respect the child labor laws," the professor said to Sir Edmund, "and give Oliver and Celia some time to rest and do their summer reading. They must get ready for the sixth grade, after all."

Sir Edmund just snorted at the professor, and then looked at Oliver and Celia.

"My plane is fueling now. We'll leave right away." He turned and left the room with an angry wave of his arms.

Dr. Navel rushed to his children and dropped to one knee in front of them.

"I'm sorry I couldn't protect you from this," he said, and he was crying. "I swear, when you get back, you can watch whatever you like. I won't make you come to a Ceremony of Discovery ever again."

"Deal," said Celia. "You owe us big-time."

"Things will be back to normal soon," he promised. "Work hard this summer. Sir Edmund can't hurt you right now. Not with everyone watching. And maybe when you get back, I will have found your mother."

"Oh, Dad," Celia said. "I don't think she wants to be found."

He didn't answer her, just hugged her again and hugged Oliver.

"Good luck," he said.

"You too," said Oliver.

"Remember what I told you," Professor Rasmali-Greenberg called out.

"Remember the premium channels," Celia responded.

The explorers stepped out of Oliver and Celia's way as they passed, making a path to the door.

"What now?" Oliver whispered, slinging the backpack onto his back. "Do we run?"

"No," said Celia. "What would Agent Zero do?"

"Call his stunt double," Oliver answered as

they left the Explorers Club and climbed into the big black limousine.

Sir Edmund sat directly across from them, still wearing his tuxedo from the ceremony. On his lap sat a lizard the size of a small dog. It had on a purple collar with a silver tag. The lizard was yellow and brown and studded with hard little bumps that looked like armor. It had a flat face and an expression like it just ate a raw onion. It smelled like it too.

"Celia and Oliver," Sir Edmund said. "This is Beverly." He reached over and plopped the lizard right onto Oliver's lap. Her claws curled and gripped onto his leg. Oliver winced but didn't want to show Sir Edmund that he was in pain.

"She is a *Heloderma horridum*, which means, basically, horrible armor. You'll be responsible for looking after her now. She gets very nervous when she travels."

"Where are we going?" Celia said.

"Oh, you'll see soon enough," answered Sir Edmund. "I think you'll find it . . . educational." He laughed and popped a fried beetle into his mouth.

The lizard stared up at Oliver's face, flicking her tongue.

"Ummm, does she . . . ummm . . . bite?" Oliver asked.

"Oh, I hope not," said Sir Edmund. "She's horribly poisonous."

Oliver went pale as the doors locked and the limo sped away toward what was going to be a very long summer with a very big lizard.

# A NOTE FROM THE AUTHOR

It is my duty to inform you, before we meet again on Oliver and Celia's next adventure, that some of what you have just experienced with the Navels is entirely true.

There really is an Explorers Club in New York City much like the one I have described, and although they are not the same, its banquets are perhaps more strange than this tale has revealed. The real one is not actually on Seventy-fourth Street and no one lives on the 4½th floor. They do, however, possess a stuffed bear.

There really is a group of Poison Witches somewhere in Tibet who prey on the unsuspecting traveler, though their criminal ways have nothing to do with the Bön religion. There really are oracles and sky burials in Tibet and the Lost Tablets of Alexandria did exist, though some have found their way into museums. The existence of the yeti has never been confirmed and I have not yet met a talking yak, nor visited Shangri-La, but since I do not have access to the secret files of the Explorers Club, I can't state for certain that they do not exist.

I am leaving it to you, the daring reader, to determine the rest of what is true and what is false.

Please let us know as soon as possible what you discover.

Send old-fashioned letters to:

C. Alexander London
*Care of: Philomel Books*
345 Hudson Street
New York, NY 10014 USA

Or write us an e-mail, report your discoveries, and track Oliver and Celia's adventures by visiting:
www.calexanderlondon.com

# ABOUT THE AUTHOR

**C. ALEXANDER LONDON** is an award-winning author of nonfiction for grown-ups, an accomplished skeet shooter, a master scuba diver, and a fully licensed librarian. He has watched television in twenty-three countries and survived an erupting volcano, a hurricane, four civil wars, and a mysterious bite on his little toe in the jungles of Thailand. Currently, C. Alexander London lives in Brooklyn, New York.

www.calexanderlondon.com